204

Dear Frien

Enter the Circle of Love—and travel to faraway places with romantic heroes . . .

We read hundreds of novels and, each month select the very best—from the finest writers around the world—to bring you these wonderful love stories . . . stories that let *you* share in a variety of beautiful romantic experiences.

With Circle of Love Romances, you treat yourself to a romantic holiday—anytime, anywhere. And because we want to please you, won't you write and let us know your comments and suggestions?

Meanwhile, welcome to the Circle of Love—we don't think you'll ever want to leave!

Best,

Cathy Camhy
Editor

CIRCLE OF LOVE™

Heron's Keep

Samantha Clare

BANTAM BOOKS
TORONTO · NEW YORK · LONDON · SYDNEY

HERON'S KEEP

A Bantam Book/June 1982

CIRCLE OF LOVE, the garland and the ring designs are
trademarks of Bantam Books, Inc.

ISBN 0-553-21513-2

Published simultaneously in the United States and Canada

Bantam Books are published by Bantam Books, Inc. Its
trademark, consisting of the words "Bantam Books" and the
portrayal of a rooster, is Registered in U.S. Patent and
Trademark Office and in other countries. Marca Registrada.
Bantam Books, Inc., 666 Fifth Avenue, New York, New York
10103.

PRINTED IN THE UNITED STATES OF AMERICA

0 9 8 7 6 5 4 3 2 1

One

"Heron's Keep," repeated the shoplady, regarding Jenna with sudden interest, "Aye, I ken it fine, it's a grand place, but it's a goodish way and you'll have to go over the Devil's Pass. You should have taken the main road."

"I prefer the side roads," Jenna told her, "but the Devil's Pass sounds rather formidable. Is it something to be avoided?"

"It's no so bad in good weather, but in a mist like this—" she glanced out of the window at the grey shroud that blanketed the view. "Well, *I* wouldn't attempt it."

"What is it—a mountain pass?"

"Aye. The road winds between the heads of the ben at first, but in places further on there are sheer drops to the sea below."

Jenna stared at her in dismay. "Oh, dear!" she murmured. "I'll have to go. I must be there this afternoon, and to go back to join the main road again would take too long."

"Now, now, Peggy, you make it sound desperate, which it is not. Don't I travel it every day of my life?"

Both women turned to look at the man who had been listening silently to their exchange.

"Jaimie here drives the post bus," explained the woman.

"I'd take you there myself, but for the fact that I'm

7

away to collect the mail," he said to Jenna. "But don't you let Peggy worry you. There's nothing to it. Just a few bends and twists, and views to gladden the heart."

"Not in this weather," Peggy pointed out.

"Well, perhaps not at the moment," he conceded, "but it'll brighten up soon. The sun will break through before midday. See if I'm not right." And nodding to them, he picked up his letter bag and left.

"Is he usually right?" asked Jenna as the door closed behind him.

"He's better as a weather prophet than he is as a guide to the roads," she was told dryly. "Take my advice and go back, even if it does take longer."

"I'm afraid I can't."

"Friend's waiting, are they?"

Jenna shook her head, "I'm taking up a post as a secretary there. So you see I *can't* be late."

"I can see it wouldn't do, but just be a wee bittee careful on the drive."

"I will," promised the girl. "I'll take some rolls and cheese, if I may, and then I'll be all set for a picnic lunch . . . and tomatoes, if you have them."

The woman nodded and began putting together the groceries. "There's a postcard there that might interest you," she said, indicating a revolving stand on the counter.

Jenna flicked it around, glancing idly at the brightly coloured views until one caught her attention, making her heart bound with sudden recognition. The photograph had been taken at sunset; the sky was deep blue, shot through in places by orange and pink. The silhouette of a turreted castle stood out, stark and black, against the background, while below at the base of a rocky cliff, long, slow waves lapped at smooth, silver sand.

"It's beautiful!" she breathed.

8

"It is that. If only it was open to the public, tourists would be flocking there, but it's privately owned and still lived in, as no doubt you know."

Jenna shook her head. "I don't know anything about the family living there now—but I do know from books that it's an old MacKenzie stronghold."

"That's right, miss. I daresay it's seen many a bloody battle in its time."

Jenna paid for her groceries and bought a post-card of the castle. Thanking the shoplady, she left. Remembering the postman's prophecy, she had hoped that the mist might have cleared, instead of which she was dismayed to find that, if anything, it had grown thicker while she had been in the village shop. She had left Fort William in gentle rain, the landlady of the boarding house where she had stayed the night assuring her that such a morning meant better weather later, but it seemed that she, too, was wrong.

Hurrying through the damp air, she threw her purchases onto the back seat of her yellow Mini and climbed behind the wheel, pausing a moment while she looked out at the depressing scene before her and contemplated the wisdom of going on. One glance at her watch told her plainly that if she was to arrive at her destination before evening, she had no choice and, somewhat reluctantly, started the en-gine and edged cautiously out of the tiny car park. Only her determination to live and work at Heron's Keep had made her undertake the long and difficult journey, and having almost arrived at the culmina-tion to all her hopes and schemes she was not prepared to lose the opportunity at this point.

Regretting the decision that had made her turn off the main road so many miles back, she drove out of the cluster of low houses and followed the sign post pointing to the Devil's Pass.

Once out of the village the road rose steadily, but

she had not realized the gradient until the mist parted momentarily and she caught a horrifying glimpse of a rushing river, and rocks and boulders far below her. Then the obscuring curtain closed in again, and she could only see the narrow road for a few feet ahead.

The monotonous sweep of the windshield wipers began to play on her stretched nerves, and when a car horn honked noisily behind her, she started and swerved wildly across the damp road. Glancing in her driving mirror, she saw a big, old car crowding on her tail, the brightly painted shark's teeth on its hood almost touching the yellow paint of her Mini. The youths in the front seat gestured wildly to her to get out of their way, while the overcrowded back seat seemed to be filled to capacity with jean-clad bodies.

Frowning, Jenna looked for a passing place, unhappily aware that no one could overtake with safety until the road widened. The driver behind honked again and swung out, trying to draw along-side her. For her own safety, Jenna was forced to step harder on the accelerator and the little car forged valiantly ahead, but soon the steep gradient told on the small engine. Slowly she began to drop back again, and the car behind caught up with her.

More imperious tooting and emphatic gestures told her that they were still determined to pass her and, biting her lip, she felt her mouth go dry with fear at the thought of being run off the road and over the cliff edge. Having reached one summit, the road dropped suddenly, curving between boulders and clumps of grass. The following vehicle, with its heavy load, gathered momentum and to her horror seemed to be nudging at her rear.

At last they reached the bottom, crossed over a narrow bridge and Jenna had a quick sight of sparkling, dashing water, leaping over stones and boulders before they started up the other side. The road was not so steep here, but required more maneuvering to negotiate the tight bends, and the older car did not fall back as it had done before. Missing a gear change, Jenna felt the Mini waver and her heart leapt before the engine caught and the little car edged slowly forward again.

Each hairpin bend seemed worse than the previous one and Jenna began to feel as though she was on some never-ending roller coaster. Perspiration had broken out on her upper lip, and her arms trembled with the effort of controlling and steering the car. Fright had made her heart beat faster and when she became aware of a strange panting sound, it took her some time to realize that she was making it herself.

At last, after what seemed a lifetime, she reached a flat length of road with a small car park built out over the cliff edge and, sighing with relief, she swung the Mini off the road. With a triumphant hooting and derisive gestures from the occupants, the pursuing car flashed past and Jenna switched off the engine, before collapsing weakly over the steering wheel. For a while the sound of her thudding heart filled her ears, but gradually she grew aware of the raucous calls of circling gulls and the dull, rhythmic surging of the sea below.

Slowly she opened her eyes and looked around, releasing her grip on the wheel with hands that ached and shook. Winding down the window, she was surprised to feel a wind on her hot face and, to her amazement, the mist suddenly moved and, while she watched, lifted, swirled and was gone. Blinking in the glare of brilliant sunshine, Jenna gazed at a view of breathtaking beauty. Emerald turf covered the surrounding mountains like green velvet, grey rocks shimmered and sparkled with the twinkling residue of the recent mist, while below the most intense sea she had ever imagined, lashed against the base of precipitous cliffs. And all around, myriad seabirds dipped and called, hovering effortlessly on the fresh Atlantic breeze.

Impulsively, she opened the door and stepped out on trembling legs, pulling the ribbon from her hair and running fingers through the long, thick strands. The wind snatched at her, and Jenna leaned into it, letting the elements take away the strain of the last half hour, calming her nerves and soothing away her tension.

"Well," she remarked to herself, "who'd have thought to find hooligans in such a lovely setting?" And finding a convenient boulder, she sat on it, gazing out to sea until she had quite recovered from her alarming experience.

Liking the place and the situation, Jenna decided to stay there and have an early lunch before resuming her journey to Heron's Keep. Even now she hardly dared believe her luck in seeing the position advertised in a magazine—and in actually obtaining the post. All her life, Heron's Keep had been the stuff of dreams and fairy tales. The ancient Scottish castle had filled her imaginings for as long as she could remember, but now she found herself almost afraid to think of it and the all-enveloping reason behind her desire to go there. Afraid she might find it was all some horrible mistake and her job already filled—or the castle itself vanished like the village in the musical "Brigadoon."

Having shared her meal with the hungry gulls, she ignored their loud demands for more and, tying her hair back again in the style which she hoped would give her the air of an efficient secretary, climbed into her car and drove out of the car park and back onto the winding road.

Ahead she could see snatches of the road vanishing and reappearing as it wound its way over the undulating mountains. On her left the brilliant azure sea sparkled and glistened until it met the distant horizon. Sighing with pleasure, Jenna wished that she could stop and admire the view, but a glance at her watch told her that she had no time to spare: she had to be content with snatched half glances as she drove. Totally immersed in her surroundings, she was unaware that a car was approaching on the narrow road ahead, until an imperious note on its horn brought back her wandering attention.

Slowing to a halt, she pulled on the hand brake and waited hopefully for the driver to back away. A few minutes later, when they had duly contemplated each other, she looked surreptitiously over her shoulder to find, as she had suspected, that a passing place lay just a few yards behind her.

With a bright smile at the driver of the car ahead she casually put on large sunglasses, hoping that he had not noticed the wider space behind her. With a sinking heart, she watched as he raised a hand and made a gentle sweeping gesture to her. Backing the car had never been her strong point. She had only passed her test after a concentrated course of backing in and out of friends' garages and drives, and since then had avoided the necessity as much as possible. The earlier events had worn her nerves to breaking point, and one glance backwards at the road sloping steeply away, with a sheer drop to the Atlantic crashing against the cliff base, was enough to bring her out in a cold sweat of fear.

Avoiding the driver's gaze, she hid behind her sunglasses and shook her head. For a few seconds there was silence, save for the seabirds mewing, and the pounding of the waves below. Then the thud of a car door closing, followed by the sound of firm footsteps approaching.

"Would you be so kind as to back into the passing place," said a cool but pleasant voice. Stealing a glance at the man bending down to speak through her open window, Jenna found herself confronting a tall, handsome man who, at any other time, she would have been pleased to meet.

"I want to get by," he said as she made no reply. "Will you back—"

"Why can't you?" Jenna demanded, more abruptly than she had intended.

Dark eyebrows snapped together in a frown, while his mouth tightened perceptibly, making her wonder if he owned the hot temper usually associated with red hair.

"My dear girl," he said, emphasizing each word, "the nearest passing place behind me is at least a mile back." He raised his eyes significantly to measure off the yards to the space behind her. "Now, do use your sense, put your car into reverse and drive back just that little way."

Lowering her chin, Jenna shook her head stubbornly. "No," she said, gripping the steering wheel tightly to control her trembling hands.

"Good God woman, what's wrong with you?" the man burst out impatiently. "We've already wasted far longer than it would have taken you to back up!"

Suddenly the car door was opened and a long leg was reaching in beside her. "Move over," he commanded briefly, and to avoid contact with him she had to scramble across the gearstick into the passenger seat in a flurry of uncoordinated movement.

"H-how dare you! Get out at once," she gasped indignantly, contemplating snatching the steering wheel from his grasp. But remembrance of the sheer drop and narrow road made her sit quietly while his strong, brown hands guided the car.

Finding reverse easily, the stranger half turned in the seat, guiding the Mini backwards skillfully. At the first movement, Jenna gasped and, closing her eyes, sat rigid with fear, expecting each moment to be precipitated over the edge of the cliff.

At last the car was still. The man switched off the engine and pulled on the hand brake. Slowly, Jenna opened her eyes and glanced fearfully about. Instead of getting out as she expected the man turned to look at her, his gaze shrewd and intent.

"Why didn't you tell me you were afraid?" he asked.

Jenna looked away, unconsciously lifting her chin. "It's not the kind of thing one wants to admit."

"Admit! My dear girl, you shouldn't be out on the road."

Stung, she turned quickly to face him. "Let me tell you, I have just driven from London," she cried, indignant at his disparagement.

"Then it must have been more by luck than skill," he said dryly, leaning one arm along the back of the seat, the better to view her flaming cheeks and sparkling eyes.

"It's none of your business, but I passed my test the first time," she went on warmly, "which is more than most people do. If I—if it hadn't been for those boys, I would have been quite all right. They made me nervous."

His gaze narrowed. "What boys?"

"The ones who drove on my tail—"

"Did you get their number?"

She shook her head. "But their car had a shark's head painted on it."

His mouth tightened grimly. "I know who they are," he said, leaving her with the impression that the youths would not escape scot-free.

"They didn't do anything, really—just followed too closely and made gestures," she felt impelled to say.

"And behaved foolishly," he finished for her and sat silent for a moment, regarding her. "I'm sorry you had to have such an introduction to the Highlands," he went on. "I only hope it won't spoil your holiday."

She opened her mouth to tell him that she was not on holiday, but at that moment he climbed out of the car, pausing to look in at the window. The sun struck bright flame from his hair, the white polo shirt he wore highlighting his lean, tanned face, making Jenna think of an illustration for the prince in a fairy story she had read as a child. She found herself blinking silently up at him.

"I still think your driving leaves much to be desired—take care on our roads," he said. And sketching a salute, he walked back to his waiting car.

"Dear me," murmured Jenna, shaken by the brief encounter. "What an impossible man! Well ... thank goodness I shan't be meeting him again."

Waiting only until he drove past with the curtest of waves, she went on, more unsettled by the day's events than she cared to admit. Suddenly the long journey palled, and she found herself longing wearily for the first sight of her destination.

Two

The sun suddenly blinded her as the car topped the hill and Jenna pulled down the vizor . . . and then, looking ahead she could see the castle. "Heron's Keep," she said the name aloud to herself and let the car speed down the steep road towards the stone building silhouetted against the bright sky.

She stopped at the base of the promontory on which it stood, and looked up. The sun made the walls appear touched with gold and, against the background of mountains behind and sea below, the castle with its many turrets rising against the sky seemed like an illustration from a French fairy tale.

Her eyes wandered over it hungrily, taking in the many windows and arches, the air of impregnability it still carried after all the years since it had been built as a stronghold for the Chief of the Mac-Kenzies. She sighed, and stretched wearily, as she recalled her childhood talks with her father and her promise to go someday to Heron's Keep, their ancestral home.

Smiling, she remembered how they had pored over maps and old books, studying anything that had to do with the history of Scotland and the MacKenzie clan. And now, she was in the depths of MacKenzie country for the first time.

Recalled from her reverie by the raucous cry of a seagull as it wheeled overhead, she started the car and drove under the curved stone archway into the courtyard of the castle. Flowers in stone urns and leaden troughs stood on the cobbles, brightening the sober effect of the grey stonework. A wide, shallow flight of stairs led up to a heavy wooden door that stood open and, after a moment, Jenna slid out of the car and climbed towards the entrance. A brass handbell stood invitingly on a table near the door, but she hesitated before stretching out her hand to ring it somewhat timidly, half-afraid to disturb the quiet of the late afternoon.

Several seconds later, when no one had appeared from the dark, cavernous depths stretching away into the interior of the castle, Jenna rubbed her hands nervously down her crumpled pants suit and looked rather helplessly about. To her left the steps continued onto a raised walk that led around the high walls surrounding the keep and, on sudden impulse, she left the doorway and headed up towards the far wall, where she could hear the rhythmic sounds of the sea.

Leaning over the warm, waist-high stones she could see the waves lapping against the base of the cliff far below. The fresh breeze was cool against her hot cheeks and she again pulled her hair free from the confining ribbon. The wind lifted the heavy masses away from her face and she tilted her head back, shaking the hair away from her neck, then stretched and flexed her shoulders, tired after the long drive.

"I really must ask you to leave," said a crisp masculine voice behind her, and Jenna turned to see a tall figure watching her.

Half-blinded by the dazzle of the bright sun and sparkling sea, she could only blink at the black silhouette while she tried to gather her startled wits.

The wind snatched at her hair, whipping it across her face and, uncomfortably aware of her disadvantage and wishing that she had kept it neat with the ribbon, she put up her hands and held the dark strands tightly against each ear.

"I'm sorry," she began, only to break off in surprise as she recognized the man confronting her.

The red head nodded slightly, but evidently he intended to make no concessions to their slight acquaintance, for his face was stern, with no sign of a smile. "I'm surprised to see you here," he said coldly. "This is a private house, you know, not a museum, nor open to the public."

"I did ring the bell, but no one came." Jenna was puzzled by his behaviour.

"Do you usually walk into people's gardens?" he went on relentlessly, his eyes sliding over her, taking in her crumpled pants suit and her general air of dishevelment.

Under his cool gaze Jenna found herself flushing slightly and wishing that she had paused to freshen herself at a hotel, as she had been half inclined to do, instead of hurrying on in her eagerness to see Heron's Keep.

"I should have recognized the car," went on the man, gesturing below. "I'd be grateful if you'd move it—once again it's blocking my way."

The girl stiffened at his disparaging tone; the little Mini might be elderly, with patches of rust showing through her bright yellow paint work, but she had bought it with her total amount of savings and took great pride in her possession . . . besides she was inclined to feel that the tiny car had made a big achievement in surmounting all the mountains and rugged country of the last few days.

Moving out of the sun, she looked with interest at the man confronting her. Unfortunately, she had to look up rather a long way, but she countered this by lifting her chin defiantly and looking scornfully at him along the length of her short nose.

"Are you usually so rude," she asked sweetly, "or is it just that you have had a bad day?"

He looked startled, and a gleam that could have been interest showed in his grey eyes, while the sun behind touched his hair to a halo of flame. One eyebrow lifted as he looked down at her.

"Would you be so kind as to move your car— *again?*" he asked with exaggerated politeness.

"What shall I do with it?"

"My dear girl, why ask me? Drive off in it, I suppose!"

"I *am* expected, you know," Jenna put in quietly and turned away to contemplate the sea.

"Expected!" There was a moment's stunned silence. "You must be Miss Clair. I thought you were a tourist, we have a plague of them at the moment. I expected someone much older . . . you must forgive me."

The words were flung at her conventionally, but Jenna knew that it was a matter of indifference to him whether she accepted his apology or not.

He looked her over critically. "You are hardly what I expected."

She flushed, knowing that in her letters she had carefully avoided all mention of her age, concentrating on her qualifications. "You didn't ask for a photograph," she pointed out, while realizing with a sinking heart, that this man must be her new employer and that she had hardly made a good start with him. "I take it that you are Mr. Trent?" she asked miserably.

"Yes, I'm Ross Trent," he said, adding as though reading her thoughts. "We have hardly met under auspicious circumstances, have we?" He took in her rather forlorn appearance and went on in a kinder tone, "However I hope we'll get along quite well."

Jenna doubted it. Ross Trent struck her as an overbearing, unsympathetic figure for an employer, but she said nothing, following him dutifully as he led the way to her car.

"Swing it around to the left and one of my men will put it away later," he said as she slid into the driving seat and started the engine under his watchful gaze.

Her driving test only three months past, Jenna still found driving required all of her attention and she found his cool grey eyes unnerving to say the least. She gritted her teeth when the gears grated as they hadn't done since she was learning. Even so, she would have managed well enough had not a perverse wind sneaked in the open window and sucked a thick strand of hair across her eyes. The car snapped into gear and shot backwards much faster than she intended. A thud and crash behind told her, without the need to look, that she had hit one of the floral urns that were placed about the courtyard. Involuntarily, she shuddered and closed her eyes.

Unwillingly, she looked up at Ross Trent's impassive face as he opened the car door. "Out," he commanded curtly, and she scrambled to obey him, watching in silence as he swung the car around effortlessly and parked it neatly against the far wall, before driving his own car in from the road.

"You must let me give you lessons," he said, tossing the keys to her. Then, taking her elbow in a firm grip, he led her up the steps and into the house.

Feeling a prisoner, Jenna would have given much to pull free from the restraining fingers, but a quick glance at the implacable face so far above hers made her feel that it would be useless.

After the bright sunshine outside, the interior

seemed almost nightdark and she hesitated on the threshold until urged on by the grip on her arm. Blinking, she found herself in a huge hall. Checkered stone tiles covered the floor, blackened wood beams arched overhead, while the paneled walls were covered with crossed weapons and ancient targes* and banners. A mournful stag's head glowered at her from the first landing of a shallow staircase that led up and then divided into two before it joined a gallery that ran around the upper walls.

"Mrs. Frazer," called the man beside her, apparently unaware of the effect the splendour had upon the girl. In answer to his voice, a small, stout woman bustled out of the shadows beside the staircase and hurried towards them, eyeing Jenna inquisitively. "Some tea, Mrs. Frazer, and then ask Munroe to garage Miss Clair's car and take her luggage up to her room."

"Aye. It's all ready—I've been expecting her the day."

"Well, at least someone expected you," Ross Trent said, opening a door and gesturing for her to go in.

White plastered walls reflected the sun outside and after the splendid gloom of the hall, the room was a blaze of light and colour. Gay chintz covered the huge comfortable sofa and chairs, small bright pictures hung on the walls. Dainty walnut furniture stood about, arranged in attractive groups, while red silk curtains swayed in the breeze from the long windows that stood open onto a wide terrace.

Jenna exclaimed in delight, "What a lovely room!"

Mr. Trent turned to look down at her. "More to your liking than the hall?" he asked quizzically.

---

*a light, circular shield or buckler

"It's—beautiful."

"My mother made it," he explained simply, but she caught an underlying note of pride in his voice. "Shall we have our tea here, or out on the balcony?"

"Outside, please—I've been cooped up in the car all day."

Weariness crept into her voice and he looked up, noting the signs of tiredness about her. "Tea—and then Mrs. Frazer can show you your room," he said more kindly than he had yet spoken.

The housekeeper entered at that moment, carrying a large tray with silver and china laid on it. At a word from Ross Trent, she carried it outside and set it down on a wicker table, before withdrawing quietly.

"Milk?" he asked, pouring a stream of steaming golden liquid into the shallow, thin cups. At the shake of her head, he handed the cup to her, gesturing for her to help herself to the plate of wafer-thin sandwiches and homemade cakes.

Jenna found herself surprisingly hungry, and ate eagerly, noting the while that her employer did not eat, himself, seeming to prefer watching her lazily as he leaned back against the cushions in his wicker chair.

"You must have realized from the wording in my advertisement that I wanted an older woman than you for my secretary," he said at last, making her hastily swallow the rest of her tea. "Why did you deliberately deceive me?"

Jenna sat her cup back onto the table, carefully avoiding his eyes. Ever since she had applied for the position she had known that this question must come, and had decided that a half truth might serve to answer it.

"I have very good qualifications . . . and I've always longed to visit Scotland. Scottish history was a great

23

interest of my father's . . . we used to talk a lot . . ."

Something desolate in her voice made him eye her intently. "Your father is . . . ?"

"He died last year," she supplied bleakly.

"And your mother?"

"She died when I was born."

He did not offer conventional sympathy, but after a moment went on, "We'll overlook the method you used to gain employment here—if you are as competent as you say you are, we should get on well together. You realize that the position is only for six months? I'm writing the history of Heron's Keep, and I imagine that is how long it will take me. I take it that you share your father's interest in Scottish history?"

"Oh, yes."

He smiled at her eagerness and, for the first time she saw his somewhat hard expression relax. "Good. Then we'll start tomorrow." He reached out a long arm and touched a bell. "Mrs. Frazer will show you to your room."

Jenna stood up, shyly brushing crumbs from her lap and then flicked her heavy hair back over her shoulders.

"Ah, Mrs. Frazer," said Ross Trent as his housekeeper entered. "I believe Miss Clair is tired. Perhaps you will arrange for her to have a tray in her room tonight?"

Just how tired she was Jenna realized as she climbed the stairs behind the sturdy Scots woman.

"Do we dress for dinner?" she asked diffidently.

The older woman looked back. "Aye," she answered briefly, and proceeded along the gallery to open a door at the far end.

Again, after the gloom of the hall, Jenna was unprepared for the brightness of the room ahead. White painted walls enhanced the delicate dark furniture, pale green silk curtains hung at the deep windows cut into the thick walls of the castle, and the bed's elegant four posts held up a cloud of thin, white muslin.

Mrs. Frazer waited, one hand on the door latch, while the girl took in her surroundings. "We call it the Lady's Room," she said.

"Which lady?" asked Jenna quickly.

"Och, one of the MacKenzies forbye. The bathroom's through there," she nodded towards a door in one of the walls. "I'll have a tray sent up in about an hour—breakfast is at eight-thirty. Should you want anything there's a bell by the bed."

"Yes . . . thank you." Jenna watched as the door closed and then, suddenly exultant, spun around and around on her toes. She had done it! She was in the castle of the MacKenzies at last!

Three

Jenna awoke quickly and lay for a minute, taking in her unfamiliar surroundings, before noticing a tray of tea beside the bed and realizing that it must have been the sound of the door closing that had disturbed her.

Pale sunlight was finding its way in at the deep-set windows, but the room was still a haven of half light and Jenna sat up, eager to think over the events of the preceding day—a thing she had been too tired to do the previous night.

Brought up on tales of Trent treachery, tales that had no doubt grown with each telling, she had come quite prepared to dislike Ross Trent. She found the thought of pitting her wits against him exhilarating and looked forward to the coming events with interest. She was determined to unravel the mystery surrounding Heron's Keep—for though no one but herself might know it, mystery there was. Over a hundred years ago, her ancestress, Silis MacKenzie, had fled the castle, taking only a few possessions with her. And, although Silis had been the sole heiress in her own right, the Trents, an English family, appeared to have taken over all her holdings, seemingly without opposition. The burning ambition of Jenna's father had been to save enough money to take the matter to court and claim his inheritance—an ambition never fulfilled. But now his daughter was prepared to enter the fray, and when she had seen the advertisement in the paper for a secretary at Heron's Keep, it had seemed like a Godsent opportunity. That she had obtained the post and actually was in the Scottish castle, she could hardly believe.

All the tales had told of the 'MacKenzie's Luck'—a magical stone that held the fortunes of the family in its cold grasp. It had vanished with the Lady Silis, and ever since she was a child all Jenna's daydreams had involved finding the precious stone—at which moment the castle would be magically returned to its ancient owners.

While she no longer felt that it would be quite as easy as her childish imaginings, Jenna still determined to find the 'Luck'—if only for the satisfaction of confronting Ross Trent with it.

She finished her tea and jumped out of bed, curling her toes in the luxury of the thick pile of the cream carpet that covered the floor before she ran across to the windows. They were set in two identical alcoves which were almost like tiny rooms themselves, with a table and chair in one and a small bookcase in the other. Jenna knelt on the wooden windowseat and, opening the casement, leaned out. Far below, a shallow sea sucked and swirled among seaweed-covered rocks and, across the expanse of the sea loch, mountains showed hazily through the early morning mist. The girl gazed in delight, drinking in the beauty of a scene that, until then, she had only imagined. A sound below made her look down, and she saw that the terrace where she had sat the day before continued around this part of the castle, and that Ross Trent leaned against the surrounding waist-high wall. His head was tilted back and he was obviously watching her.

Seeing she had noticed him, he raised a hand in

ironical salute. "Good morning, Miss Clair," he called. "Don't catch cold."

Jenna flushed and put a hand to her neck, suddenly aware that she was wearing only a flimsy nightdress. Hurriedly, she withdrew her head, closing the window rather smartly behind her, but not before a sound suspiciously like a chuckle had floated up to her ears.

The night before, she had wondered what a bathroom in such a setting would be like, half inclined to imagine that it would have huge porcelain and brass fittings like something in a museum. But she discovered that it was surprisingly normal, if not luxurious: only the green sunken bath provided an exotic touch. At any other time she would have delighted in spending hours in the hot, scented water—after a lifetime of boarding house baths with lukewarm water and waiting queues outside the door, her own bathroom was a luxury to be enjoyed. But her eagerness to begin the day and, perhaps, the task of finding the 'Luck' made her hurry.

Remembering Mr. Trent's disparaging eyes, she chose her dress with care, settling at last for a simple green linen and white shoes. She tied back her hair with a white scarf.

She found her way to the hall and was hesitating over which of the many doors would lead into the breakfast room, when she was joined by a young man who suddenly appeared at her side, bringing the smell of peat and heather with him.

"Hallo," he said, stopping and examining her with interest. "You must be Miss Clair. I'm Alex Trent, Ross's brother. I expect you're looking for something to eat."

Jenna shook hands and looked at him covertly as he swept her into a room on the other side of the hall. Not as tall as his brother, he gave the impression of being much younger and less intimidating. Catching her eye, he grinned and she found herself smiling back, suddenly feeling much happier.

"I see you've met Miss Clair," observed Ross Trent, folding his paper and looking up as they entered.

"I found her hovering in the hall."

"There are so many doors—I felt a bit like Alice!"

Penetrating grey eyes studied her. "No need to be nervous, Miss Clair, we don't have a dragon waiting for its meal of maidens—or even a family ghost."

"Perhaps they all left with the MacKenzies," Jenna said, and was aware at once that she had made a mistake.

His eyes narrowed. "What do you mean?"

"Only that . . . this is MacKenzie country and that Heron's Keep must have belonged to them once."

He looked as if he would reply, but Alex cut across their talk.

"No more history, not at breakfast," he pleaded. "Ever since Ross decided to write the history of the place, we've heard nothing else." He leaned closer and said in mock confidence, "Mind you, I don't mind if it brings new blood to the scene. I've a few letters you could take down for me."

"Miss Clair is my sole property," came his brother's cool voice. "She works for me—and no one else."

"Not even Carla? I'll lay a wager that she will find a few jobs to be done."

"Not even Carla."

Jenna pricked up her ears at the mention of this unknown woman, and found herself looking across the table inquiringly.

"Carla Van Damm is our cousin," supplied Alex, "from America."

"Her grandmother and ours were sisters," explained Ross Trent. "So we are more kinfolk than actual cousins."

29

"Well, whatever she is as a relative—she's quite something."

"I'll look forward to meeting her," Jenna said, privately wondering what this American would be like.

"We all have coffee in the balcony room about eleven," said Ross. "You will meet her then. Carla can never face the day until she's breakfasted in bed. I'm glad to see that you have no objections to early rising."

Jenna smiled. "Last week I would have been well on my way to work by now—after cooking my own breakfast and doing a few chores."

"I'd forgotten that you are a working woman," said Ross, and she heard the faint mockery in his voice.

"Are you one of those bachelor girls who live an emancipated life in a flat of their own?" asked his younger brother curiously.

Thinking of the tiny bed-sitter, Jenna had to smile at the life Alex was obviously imagining for her. "I lived alone," she agreed, "but it could hardly be called a flat—more of a cupboard! And I never had time to do more than boil an egg in the mornings. My breakfasts were never as delicious as these herrings."

She reluctantly declined Alex's offer of oatcakes and marmalade and, as though he had been waiting, Ross dropped his napkin back on the table and stood up.

"If you've finished, Miss Clair, I'll show you where we'll be working."

She followed his tall form into the hall and along a passage into a part of the castle where the rooms were smaller and obviously furnished for working.

"The kitchens are along there," said her guide, nodding towards a long passage that led off at an angle. "This is where I work," he touched a door, "and this is your room." He opened the door and held it for her.

It was very different from the other, more opulent rooms she had seen so far and Jenna took in the sensible, large desk, electric typewriter and wall of cupboards and filing cabinets.

"It's—very businesslike," she ventured at last.

"What did you expect, Miss Clair? A rickety table and obsolete typewriter? I'm a businessman and I know that a worker is as good as his tools. I expect my workers to be very good indeed."

"I'll have to be very good to keep up with that monster," she said feelingly.

Her employer reached past her and, opening a drawer, took out a thin booklet which he dropped on the desk. "The instructions that came with it," he said. "They seem quite simple."

"I'll do my best to understand them," said Jenna, deceptively demure.

"I'm sure you will." For a moment their eyes met in what under other circumstances might have been a challenge, then Ross Trent nodded slightly. "Coffee at about eleven," he said before leaving the room.

Left alone, Jenna inspected her surroundings before turning her attention to the gleaming machine on the desk. Sitting down to read the instructions in the pamphlet, she found to her relief that the workings of the typewriter were comparatively simple and soon her fingers were flying over the keys. Practicing until she felt competent, the hours passed quickly and she was surprised to find that it was almost eleven when she looked at her wrist watch. Remembering the command to take coffee in the balcony room, she tidied her desk, before setting out to find her way back into the living quarters of the castle.

The room was as delightful as she remembered it and she stood on the threshold for a second, before crossing the floor to where a tray was set for coffee on a low table between two huge, squashy sofas. At her approach, Alex came to his feet, smiling easily.

"Carla, may I introduce Miss Clair? Miss Clair—Miss Van Damm."

"Oh, the little secretary girl," said a lazy voice from the depths of one of the sofas and Jenna found herself subjected to a wide-eyed stare.

One glance and she knew that Alex had been right when he described Carla as 'quite something'. Long, slim legs emerged from a deceptively simple cream dress and golden hair fell like a burnished cap about a tanned, beautiful face. All at once Jenna felt small and insignificant, and she shivered slightly under the cool, blue gaze.

"How do you do," she murmured, and fell silent while Alex poured coffee and made sure she was comfortable.

"Have you been to Scotland before?" he asked offering her a plate of biscuits.

"No—never, though I've always wanted to."

"Then why didn't you?" asked Carla in puzzled tones.

Jenna looked at her, taking in the expensive clothes and jewelry. "I couldn't afford it," she said simply. "And the opportunity didn't arise."

"Of course—I forgot you are a working girl. How inconvenient it must be—to be always at someone's beck and call."

"Aren't we all?" asked Jenna lightly. "Even if it's only a relative who needs us."

Carla's elegant eyebrows were raised. "I please myself," she assured her listeners loftily.

Jenna's ready temper rose but, remembering her position, she refused the challenge so obviously offered and bit back the retort that rose to her lips, uneasily aware of the triumph in the American girl's wide-eyed gaze. For a moment she received an unblinking stare, then Carla turned to Alex, holding out her cup, but Jenna was chillingly aware that antagonism had flared in the bright room.

"I believe I told you that Miss Van Damm is our cousin?" said Alex, seeming unaware of any tension in the atmosphere.

"Yes—weren't your grandmothers sisters?"

"Grandmother Amy and Great-Aunt Katie were heiresses," supplied Carla. "At the turn of the century it was fashionable for our wealthy families to marry their daughters into the English nobility."

Jenna realized that the explanation was to point out the differences in their situations, and hugged the knowledge to herself that she was descended from the real owners of Heron's Keep.

"You Colonials are always boasting about your antecedents," said a voice and they realized that Ross Trent had come in unnoticed.

Jenna expected Carla to take umbrage, but she laughed huskily, patting the seat beside her invitingly.

"We have to make the most of what we have," she said. "You mustn't begrudge us a little history, you know."

"You can have any of mine you have a care for," declared Ross gallantly.

"Beware—I might take the most interesting and then where would you be?" Carla's blue eyes turned to Jenna and she said guilelessly, "Miss Clair, we mustn't leave you out. Have you any interesting ancestors?"

"None that I know of," answered Jenna calmly, well aware that Miss Van Damm obviously expected her to have none.

33

"But your name is interesting," put in Ross quietly. "Clair is unusual surely? Do you know where it comes from?"

She shook her head. "Not really—I know there's a place in Ireland, but that is spelt without an I."

"Oddly enough, there's a Glen Clair near here."

Her eyes flew to his face and then she lowered her gaze quickly not wanting to let him see the blaze of excitement she was feeling. For a moment, her family tales and the mystery centered around Heron's Keep seemed very near. She longed to ask more but knew that she must not arouse suspicion by showing too great an interest.

Unnoticed, the conversation flowed over her, while her mind was busy with her private thoughts. Suddenly Ross Trent stood up and she realized that coffee time was over. She thought he looked at her curiously but he said nothing as they walked back together to their workrooms . . . and then Jenna was alone and could sit at her desk, her brain a whirl of confused thoughts.

Four

Lunch was a cold meal left ready by Mrs. Frazer and taken at the time most convenient for the diners. Finding the dining room empty, Jenna filled her plate with salmon and salad and went out onto the terrace, determined not to lose a moment of the brilliant sunshine. With a gentle breeze stirring her hair, she sighed with contentment, wondering how anyone could ever be persuaded to leave such an idyllic setting.

As she poured herself a cup of coffee, Carla emerged from the doorway, eyed her thoughtfully for a moment and, having filled her own plate, came to join her.

"Alex tells me that we have one thing in common, Miss Clair," she said, spreading her napkin across well-cut linen trousers.

"Really?" Jenna heard herself saying doubtfully.

"Why, yes—we both live in an apartment in town."

Jenna laughed a little. "It seems a very grand name for my little bed-sitter."

"What exactly is a bed-sitter?"

"A room with a hidden bed, a table and chair, and the means of cooking and washing up in a corner."

Carla made no effort to hide her disdain. "Mine is a little bigger, honey," she drawled. "In fact, I guess you could just about put your bed-sitter into my living room and my maid wouldn't even notice. Of course, a big place like that takes some keeping up. Do you know my decorators told me I needed two hundred yards of material just for drapes?" She waved a disparaging hand. "I just gave them free rein and came away until it was all finished. I can't bear to be uncomfortable."

Agreeing dryly that she never cared for decorating either, Jenna remarked upon the taste and beauty of the interior of Heron's Keep.

"It sure is a show place," enthused the American girl. "My friends just love it when I tell them that my cousin owns a real Scottish castle. Of course we're not exactly cousins—kissin' kin we'd call it in the States." She smiled reflectively. " 'Course it can be a whole lot nicer—not being too close, if you know what I mean."

Jenna finished her coffee and stood up. "I must go and finish my typing," she said.

"Don't let me keep you," smiled Carla. "I know how it is with you working girls—always at your employer's beck and call."

"Two hundred yards for drapes!" muttered Jenna explosively, marching down the corridor to her workroom. "Maids—apartments—working girls— ugh!"

Eyeing the shining typewriter with frowning dislike, she hesitated, knowing she would be unable to settle to any work until she had calmed down. With sudden resolution she left the room and headed in the direction of a dark, tempting passage that led off beyond the kitchen area.

Cool and dim, with white painted walls that met overhead in a low arch, the corridor meandered past several openings and doors, none of which seemed particularly interesting—or the type in which archives and historical papers would be kept. With no very clear idea in her mind, except that she might possibly find some reference to the Lady Silis,

Jenna wandered on, peering into tiny, empty rooms and store cupboards and walking down seemingly endless hallways, until she was brought up short by the sudden realization that she was lost. With the knowledge came an unexpected attack of claustrophobia, making her glance uneasily at the low ceiling over her head while remembering that she had not seen a window for some time. Hopefully, she began to retrace her footsteps, following the trail of lights that she had switched on in passing. Several false starts ended when she walked the length of a corridor only to be met by blackness when she opened the door at the end of it. Returning and trying another direction added to her growing unease, and soon she was more nervous than she cared to admit. Wild legends of people being lost underground to wander forever filled her mind with alarming possibilities and, involuntarily, her steps quickened until she was almost running. Suddenly she found herself in a wider, better-lit passage and, turning a corner precipitously, cannoned against a body moving in the opposite direction. If a pair of strong arms had not caught and held her, she would have fallen and for a moment she allowed herself to lie against his chest while she regained her breath.

"You're not the monster of the labyrinth, are you?" she asked in a voice that shook a little, and then she dared to look up.

"No monster, only the younger brother and he's usually the hero," Alex assured her, and held her in a comforting grip until she had recovered. "What happened?" he asked, as she withdrew herself a little.

"I—got lost," she confessed shakily. "I couldn't find the way back to the workroom and I'm afraid I got frightened. You must think me very silly."

"Not at all—these old places can be very alarming to anyone who doesn't know them."

Taking her arm, he led her towards the sound of cheerful voices and the clanking of crockery, and soon the familiar sight of the workroom door came into view. Ross turned as they entered, his eyebrows lifting.

"We quite thought you had decamped, Miss Clair," he remarked, dropping the papers he had been examining back on the pile.

"Were you looking for me? I'm sorry—I'm afraid I got lost."

Jenna was afraid that he would not accept her explanation as readily as his brother and watched with dismay the sudden lift of his mobile brows.

"You surprise me," he said, and left an inviting silence.

"I hope it was all right," she said at last. "I went exploring. I do hope you don't mind. I intended to be only a few minutes, but I lost my way and all the passages looked alike."

"The poor girl was having an attack of the jitters when I found her," said Alex. "Mind you, those old underground corridors can be pretty frightening. Do you remember how we used to play there, Ross? We must show them to Carla. I'm sure she'd be interested to see a set of genuine dungeons."

The idea seemed to hold little appeal for the older man. "Why don't you ask her?" he suggested. "In the meantime, Miss Clair and I have some business."

"Oh, busy are you? I'll push off then, before you have me looking up dates and things. I had enough history at school."

Ross Trent waited until his brother's footsteps had died away before taking the girl's arm in a purposeful grip. "Come along," he said. "I find I've an hour to spare." Swooping up her big hold-all he tossed it towards her. "I presume your car keys are in there," he said, leading her to the door.

"Yes, but—where are we going . . . what do you want them for?" asked Jenna, bewildered.

"I promised you a driving lesson," Ross said, urging her down the stairs, "and now's as good a time as any."

"But—I don't need any, really. I'm quite good. I passed my test—"

"I know—first time," the man finished for her, a gleam in his eyes, "but for an incident like the one at the Devil's Pass to reduce you to a jelly—"

"A jelly!" squeaked Jenna indignantly.

"A jelly, Miss Clair. Obviously you need more practice to make you confident, and with that in mind I intend to let you drive me this afternoon."

Jenna could think of nothing that would disturb her driving ability more and dug her heels into the shingle of the courtyard. "No, thank you," she said politely.

Still holding her elbow, Ross turned to look down at her, his eyes narrowed against the glare of the sun. "Nervous, Miss Clair?" he asked softly.

"Of course not," she assured him quickly. "I— just don't like people watching me drive."

"It's something we all have to get used to," she was told, and again his arm urged her forward, making her resist, instinctively rebelling against coercion. "Miss Clair," Ross breathed quietly into her ear, "until I am satisfied with your competence, for your own safety and that of other road users, I shall not allow you to drive. As that would be inconvenient to all, I insist upon a lesson this afternoon. Think how amused Carla, who is watching from her window, would be, and how foolish you will look, if I pick you up and carry you across to your car—which is precisely what I intend to do if you don't walk there on your own two feet."

Jenna moved nervously away from him, glowering at him from under her eyebrows, and snatched a glance up at the tower, confirming that the American girl was watching. For a moment she hesitated, but one look at the determined face above her was enough to convince her that Ross Trent was quite capable of carrying out his threat, and she capitulated abruptly. Swinging on her heels, she dragged her arm free and marched to the Mini. Plonking herself down in the driving seat, she pushed the key into the ignition with hands that trembled with anger.

"Now what?" she demanded as the man joined her.

"No racing starts or rushed gear changes, if you please. Control your temper, Miss Clair, and drive calmly and smoothly. Let me see you back out and around those two urns so that you can park against the wall. That will do nicely for a start."

Gritting her teeth Jenna started the engine, determined to surprise the annoying man beside her with her driving skill. Carefully she did as he asked, and knew a little surprise at her own competence as the Mini came to a smooth stop inches from the stones of the wall.

Smiling sweetly, she turned to her companion and lifted her eyebrows inquiringly. "Well?" she wondered.

"Surprisingly well," he answered. "It's amazing what a little temper can do to settle the nerves."

Jenna eyed him with sudden suspicion. "Did you intend to make me angry?"

"There is usually a reason behind my actions," he told her blandly. "In this case it seemed a way of helping you over the tension you feel about driving."

For a moment Jenna smouldered, before her sense of humour rose to the surface. "It certainly worked," she admitted with a laugh. "I must say I carried out your instructions very well."

"Let's see how well you get on without the aid of a

paddy." He smiled in return and for the next half hour the yellow car was guided in and out of corners, and backed and parked into impossible places—all the while Jenna's confidence growing steadily.

"Take her out into the road now," commanded Ross and, with a quick look at him, she obeyed. "Back over the Devil's Pass," he said quietly as she hesitated under the entrance arch.

Knowing better than to fling him a beseeching glance, Jenna obeyed unwillingly, her hands tightening on the steering wheel as she headed up the hill away from the castle.

"It's better to tackle it now than to let it build into a bogey," came Ross Trent's quiet voice.

"I know I should agree with you—but I don't care for the idea at *all*." She was dismayed to hear a betraying waver in her voice and concentrated fiercely on the road ahead.

A hand held her shoulder briefly, the fleeting touch surprisingly comforting. "I'm here—don't worry. I shan't make you do anything you're not capable of. Relax and try to enjoy the drive."

Gradually, over the next hour and somewhat to her surprise, Jenna found herself doing precisely that. With Ross Trent a solid secure presence at her elbow, the Pass lost much of its fearsome aspect. The gradients were still steep and sharp, but now she found herself negotiating them with increasing confidence.

"Pull in here," said Ross as they approached the car park where she had stopped before.

Obediently, she pulled on the brake and switched off the engine with a jaunty gesture before turning to him with a smile.

"You were right," she admitted. "I feel much better now—left to myself I'd never have come this way again."

"With practice you'll make a good driver," he told her. "You've only just got your license, haven't you? I think you undertook the long journey up here too soon. What with the strain of driving so far—and meeting those louts—you lost your confidence. But you'll be all right now."

"Thank you," she said shyly.

He made a deprecating gesture and opened the door. "Would you care for a walk?" he asked. "There's a track off here that crosses the headland. We'll miss tea, but there is plenty of time before dinner."

Scrambling out of the car, Jenna joined him, tying a scarf over her long hair as the now familiar wind buffeted her. The Scotsman led the way to a narrow, rough track threading like a pale ribbon across the springy turf. Sheep, heavy with wool, scattered at their approach, bleating indignant protests at having their peace disturbed by two-footed intruders. Lifting her head into the breeze, Jenna savoured the sea air laden with the clean smells of grass and wild flowers.

After a while the track left the peak and, taking a downward trend, became rougher as it edged its way around boulders and rocky outcrops. Reaching the bottom of the shallow gorge, Jenna thought the way was barred by a wide, dancing stream, but then she saw that boulders lying in its bed formed stepping stones. Seeing her doubtful expression, Ross smiled.

"Have you had enough?" he asked.

Jenna shook her head. "No—I could go on forever," she answered, not hiding her enjoyment.

Using the stones rising out of the shallow water, he strode into the middle of the stream and then held out his hand to her. Springing onto the first boulder, she felt her hand grasped firmly in a warm grip, and found to her hidden confusion that she liked the sensation. The contact only lasted a minute, and then she was across the bubbling water and safe on firm ground on the other side. Ahead the path led upwards once more, at first fairly smoothly, but near the top it became a scramble over loose stones and soft earth. Here, Ross took her arm, and she found herself grateful for the support, arriving breathless at the summit to be met by yet another vista of sea and sky.

"It seems impossible, but each view is even more beautiful than the last," she gasped.

"This is my favourite," he told her and taking her arm again, turned her slightly to the right. "Over there, beyond the first headland, is Heron's Keep."

Following his pointing finger, Jenna gazed past the grey and green of the cliffs and saw a distant silhouette of turrets and conical towers gleaming in the sun. Glancing at her companion, she surprised an expression of unconscious pride and affection on his face and was suddenly made aware how much his home meant to him.

"You love it, don't you?" she said involuntarily.

He looked down at her before returning his gaze to the distant stronghold. "It holds many happy memories," he said simply. "I had a very happy childhood and was brought up on legends about the old place—just the stuff to fire a boy's imagination. Alex and I reenacted many a bloody battle in our time."

Jenna longed to ask about the MacKenzies and how the Trents came to own the castle, but instead played safe and asked the inevitable question about Bonnie Prince Charlie.

"I don't believe he ever got this far," replied Ross, amused, "though, of course, it would be romantic if we could lay claim to a visit by the Prince. Carla would revel in it."

"I suppose every one asks the same question."

Her employer's eyes gleamed. "Only the English, Miss Clair," he drawled. "Having deposed him and his family, you all seem to suffer from a guilty conscience where he is concerned—and like him far better in retrospect than you ever did in reality."

Jenna frowned. Ignoring the faint mockery in his voice, she concentrated on the implication that held most interest for her. "Aren't you English, Mr. Trent?" she asked, shading her eyes with one hand the better to study his face.

"I'm a good Scot, Miss Clair, and proud of it," he said in a voice that brooked no argument. Then, glancing at his watch, he remarked that they must turn back or be late for dinner.

Jenna was silent on the journey back to the car, pondering on the Trents' nationality, but eventually coming to the conclusion that, having lived at Heron's Keep since the departure of the Lady Silis, they must consider themselves Scots by birth if not by name. Thoughtfully she stared out of the window as they drove back to the castle with Ross at the wheel. Passing a low, stone building thatched with brown, dry heather, she could not restrain her curiosity, turning in her seat for a backward view.

"Granny Ewen's croft," supplied her companion. "It was originally a black house, but has been given a chimney nowadays." He smiled at her expression. "Once, the fire was lit on a stone in the middle of the floor and the smoke had to find its way out of a hole in the roof, with the consequence, as you can imagine, that the interior was black with soot—added to which windows were a luxury. Hence the descriptive term 'black house.'"

"It doesn't sound too nice," Jenna ventured.

"It's quite civilized now. We built her a little bathroom a few years ago, but I'm not sure that she puts it to the accepted use—more likely she brews her medicines and simples there! She's our local wise woman. Perhaps you'd call her a white witch."

Jenna's eyes opened. "You're pulling my leg," she exclaimed, sitting up. "There aren't such things now, not even up—"

"Up here," he finished for her, as she broke off realizing what she had been about to say. "The people up here, Miss Clair, are nearer to nature than you southerners, and I dare say even now there are a few folk who would sooner pay a call on Granny Ewen than visit the doctor." He smiled slightly at her shocked expression. "I'll take you to visit her," he promised, a hint of malice in his tone. "Then you can tell your friends how you met a real Highland witch woman."

Jenna smiled dutifully, realizing that she was being teased, but privately she was not at all sure she wanted to pay such a visit, visualizing a grimey, hag-like creature. Thankfully the subject was changed by Ross as they drove under the entrance arch and parked neatly by the stone wall of Heron's Keep.

Five

That evening when Carla and the men had taken their after-dinner drinks out onto the terrace, Jenna slipped back into the balcony room. She had noticed a small, white baby grand piano in a corner and felt impelled to examine it more closely. A Paisley shawl in vivid colours covered one corner, while a framed photograph stood above the music stand, obviously placed where the player could see it. Intrigued, Jenna picked it up. Two young boys grinned up at her, the elder's arm protectively about the smaller boy's shoulders and, sitting down on the piano stool, she realized that Ross and Alex Trent's mother must have been the player.

Tobacco smoke drifted in to her. Voices and the chink of glass were carried into the silent room by the soft breeze. Tentatively she touched the ivory keys with one finger, softly picking out a tune.

"Do you play?"

Supposing herself alone, she jumped at the abrupt question and, glancing around, saw Ross Trent behind her, leaning against the window frame. He was half hidden in the evening shadows and she wondered fleetingly how long he had been there watching her.

"A . . . little," she faltered.

"Let me hear you." He came forward and switched

on a lamp beside the instrument, shedding a golden pool over them both, while the rest of the room seemed to grow darker.

"I'd rather not . . . I'm not very good."

"Shy, Miss Clair?" he taunted, his eyes flickering over her. Then, taking in her slim fingers twisting together nervously, he sat down behind her.

"Have you guessed that my mother played?" he asked quietly. "I remember how, as boys, Alex and I used to listen to her music. It's a long time since I've heard anything in this room except records. . . . I'd be very grateful, Miss Clair. . . ."

Half against her will, Jenna lifted her hands and touched the cold keys with her fingers. Tentatively at first, and then with more power as she gained confidence, she began to play. The heady excitement of Chopin filled the place and she was lost to her surroundings until light suddenly flooded the room and, in confusion, she stopped playing.

"Well," drawled the American girl, her finger still on the light switch, "we wondered what was going on in here, didn't we, Alex?"

"I didn't know Miss Clair played," he agreed.

"I imagine that there's a lot we don't know about Miss Clair," came Ross's quiet voice and for a moment Jenna wondered uneasily at his meaning.

"Say, how about some records?" asked Carla rather stridently, implying that she did not care for amateur musicians. Without waiting for an answer, she walked across to the record player and began to flip through the selections.

Soon after, Jenna was able to slip away to her room thinking the subject was closed, but her employer brought it up the next day.

Alex and Carla were out somewhere and she and Ross had had a solitary lunch and taken their coffee out onto the terrace to enjoy the sun before returning to work.

"I enjoyed your playing," the man suddenly said.

"Thank you, but I know I'm only competent. I usually don't inflict my playing on other people."

"I'd say that with practice you could become more than competent."

She smiled but shook her head deprecatingly while he went on.

"Feel free to use the piano any time."

"You're very kind—"

"I like to hear it."

Abruptly he rose to his feet and strode across to the wall, looking rather blankly out to sea. Watching, Jenna had a sudden picture of two small boys listening to their mother making music and wondered what Ross Trent had been like as a child, and what had made him into the cool, self-sufficient individual he now was.

"Miss Clair," he spoke over his shoulder, and then turned to look at her, leaning back against the wall and giving her his full attention. "I am giving a dinner party in a few days, nothing very great, just a few friends in to meet Carla ... I would be very grateful if you would play for us afterwards."

Jenna spoke the first words that came into her mind. "Oh, I couldn't—I'm not good enough!"

"Good God, woman, don't be so self-deprecating!" he exploded. "You *do* play well enough—enough to give pleasure to other people. You have a talent, so why not use it?"

She blinked up at him, feeling as though she had stroked a kitten and been bitten by a tiger. "Well . . . put like that," she said, recovering her poise, "how can I refuse?"

He laughed. "You'll play, then?"

She nodded. "Who will choose the music?" she asked.

"I think we'll compromise over that. After all, I

hardly can be aware which piece you play best—or worst."

"I'll give you a selection of my best pieces." She hesitated and then went on with a slight show of embarrassment. "Will ... will it be a very grand affair, Mr. Trent?"

"Long dresses and black ties," he told her, watching more intently than she liked.

Jenna almost squirmed under his eyes. Sometimes she felt that the cool grey gaze was dissecting her, laying bare her inmost thoughts and feelings. And now he proved how well he could read her thoughts, for he said:

"No suitable dress, Miss Clair? How could you have been expecting to need one? You'll allow me to buy you one, of course."

"No, thank you—I'd rather not—"

"I insist." His voice brooked no further argument. and, as though the matter was firmly settled, he stood up, reaching a hand to help her out of the low chair. "I think it's time you explored the castle. I believe that you've caught up with the notes I left you, and before we start working together I think it would be as well if you were acquainted with the layout of Heron's Keep. Sometimes I might want you to fetch something or verify some fact for me, and it will be more convenient if you know your way around."

He led the way along the terrace to a circular tower protruding from the main building and opened a small pointed door. "The castle was built in the early fifteenth century," he said, "during the lawless heyday of clan feuds and battles. The stairs all bend around to the left for the convenience of the right-handed MacKenzies who'd be defending them. If they'd been a left-handed clan, then they would have built them the other way about."

Jenna peered into the dark interior of the tower, feeling very disinclined to climb the narrow stairs into the blackness above. While she hesitated, Ross took her hand firmly in his.

"Come along—it's not so bad as it looks," he said and, reluctantly, she allowed him to lead her upwards.

Around and around they went for what seemed an age, each footstep planted with difficulty on the narrow, tapering stair until, giddy and breathless, Jenna arrived thankfully at the top, the dazzling sun—after the almost total dark of the tower—striking her with an almost physical force. Blinded and panting, she turned around, hands outstretched, feeling for some support in her spinning world.

Hands closed on her shoulders and she was held firmly. "Stand still," Ross commanded, "and close your eyes for a moment."

Meekly she obeyed until she could see again and, opening her eyes, found herself disquietingly near to a male chest. "I'm all right now," she said hastily, stepping back out of his grasp.

Grey eyes gleamed disconcertingly and she knew that he was laughing at her confusion. Without a word he let her go and, sliding both hands into his trouser pockets, watched as she went to the high parapet and leaned over.

"Be careful," he warned, "it's a long way down."

Peering over the wall she found how truly he spoke. This tower was the highest part of the castle, overlooking even the roof of the keep and other, smaller turrets. Below, the courtyard with its flower urns and parked cars looked like a child's toy, while the beach revealed by the receding tide was a haze of soft yellow sand and grey rock.

Up here the wind was fierce, tugging at her skirt and flapping it wildly about her legs. In spite of the sun, it was cold and she shivered involuntarily, wishing she had brought a cardigan with her. Suddenly she felt a welcome warmth and, startled, felt her employer draping his jacket about her shoulders.

Smiling her thanks, she asked if he wouldn't be cold?

"We Scots are hardy," he said with a shrug and, taking her arm, indicated various points of interest lying around the castle before bringing her inside again to show her how the interior was laid out.

After that the days passed quickly, as she settled into a daily routine of taking notes and instructions from Ross Trent in the mornings and typing them in the afternoons. The music she should play at the dinner party in a week's time was settled upon and, as no mention was made of the dress, she wondered if he had forgotten his promise to provide one. She was half inclined to be glad, although she had no dress with her suitable for a grand occasion.

She took to spending the time after tea and before dinner in practicing at the white baby grand. One evening, she became aware that Alex had come in noiselessly while she was absorbed in playing. His raised eyebrows asked silently if he was disturbing her and, at the shake of her head, he trod quietly around behind her and sat in a chair where his presence would not distract her.

"It reminds me of my mother," he said as the last notes died away and she sat still, her hands in her lap.

At his words she looked up. "That's what Ross— Mr. Trent said."

"The castle used to seem full of music at times."

"Do you miss her?" she asked sympathetically.

"I guess so—I was only six, and Ross eight years older, when she was killed in a car crash, but I remember how empty our lives suddenly seemed."

"And your father?"

"He more or less gave up this place and settled in London. But Ross and I have always liked it here. I sometimes think it's our refuge from the world."

"Surely you have no need to hide away?" she asked involuntarily, surprised that people who so obviously had everything, should feel insecure or in need of shelter.

"I failed my exams, broke a leg skiing and came here to lick my wounds . . . while Ross seems to have spent more time here since his engagement was broken off."

"Oh, I see," Jenna said slowly, digesting the fact that her employer had, until recently, been engaged, and thinking that it could explain much that was brisk and curt in his dealings with her. After all, one could hardly expect him to have much love for women at the minute.

"You won't mention it to him, will you? He's rather touchy about it."

She assured him that she wouldn't and smiled at his transparent relief. Obviously his brother was a force to be reckoned with in Alex's eyes. Apparently he was reassured because he suddenly said, "Do you mind if I call you Jenna? I know that we're a little more formal in the north than you southerners. But Miss Clair seems so severe when we're living in the same house and meet every day."

"I'd be glad to hear my name again," she said truthfully. "Miss Clair always sounds such a staid person—not like me at all really."

"Jenna it is, then . . . and you must call me Alex."

Suddenly she was happier and more at ease than she had felt since arriving at Heron's Keep. Carla viewed her with dislike she knew, and her employer was correct but usually distant. Only with Alex could she relax and lower her guard.

"Is it all right to swim anywhere here?" she asked.

"Good Lord, hasn't anyone told you?" he said quickly. "It can be dangerous, but there are places where it's safe. As you know we're built on the sea edge of a loch and the tides can be difficult. Don't ever go by yourself—but I'd be happy to show you around when you feel like it. There's a good place just below the castle. I expect you've noticed the little door in the curtain wall that leads down to it. It used to be the way provisions and visitors came when they arrived by sea."

Now he mentioned it, she remembered seeing the wave-swept remains of a stone quay and steep steps cut in the rock face.

"How about tomorrow, if you're free?"

"That would be nice—oh, no, not tomorrow! It's the dinner party." Her voice shook as she spoke, and a spasm of nervousness took tight hold of her. Her father had fostered her talent and love for music and she had often played for him and his friends. But to play for people she had never met, and in a strange house, would be very different.

Next day, Ross Trent had no work for her and Jenna offered her services to Mrs. Frazer, who had spent the last few days in the kitchen submerged in an orgy of preparations. The housekeeper, who managed with the help of two local girls, was glad of her help and soon had her undertaking the simpler tasks necessary for the success of the evening. Jenna found the work good for her nerves, and the day passed more pleasantly than she had supposed it possibly could.

At last, in the late afternoon, Mrs. Frazer shooed her away. "Time you were making yourself bonny," she said, adding mysteriously, "I doubt not that you'll find that the little folk have paid you a visit."

She would say nothing else and Jenna climbed the stairs, puzzling over her statement. Opening her door, she knew at once what the housekeeper had meant, for on the bed was a large oblong box with the name of a well-known shop on its side.

Tossing aside the lid and layers of tissue paper, Jenna lifted out a dress and held it at arm's length. Pink material shimmered in the light and, holding it against her, she turned to look in the mirror. From a tiny waist the skirt sprang out in folds to the floor. Full leg o'mutton sleeves ended in tight cuffs, with a fall of white lace. Simple and yet elegant, it was the dress every girl dreams about . . . and she quite overcame all her scruples about accepting it. Laying it carefully back on the bed she went to run her bath.

The dress fitted perfectly, making her pause to wonder how Ross Trent had known her size and, when she found a pair of pink slippers—also her size—hidden deep within the box, she wondered even more. Suiting the style to the dress, she tied the side pieces of her hair on top of her head, leaving the rest to fall in soft curls about her shoulders and, looking in the mirror, reflected that she looked like a Victorian belle setting out to her first ball.

Suddenly nervous, she paused in the gallery outside her room, one hand on the latch, and would have turned tail and retreated inside again when she heard another door opening and her employer's voice halted her.

"Good evening, Miss Clair." He came nearer, taking in her appearance, a rather startled expression on his face. She thought he looked like one of his own ancestors, in the elegant dinner suit, with snowy frills at his wrists and shirt front. The light overhead struck fire from his hair and drew sparks from the diamond shirt studs.

Jenna smiled weakly, wondering why she had never realized before how handsome he was, and lifted her chin a little as he continued to examine her.

"Very nice," he approved. "You grace the frock."

Startled at the unexpected compliment, she glanced at him and then, on sudden impulse, dropped into a deep curtsey. "Thank you, sir," she said demurely.

Responding to her mood, he bowed gravely and offered her his hand with old world courtesy. Tucking her fingers under his elbow, he led her downstairs to where Carla and Alex already awaited the arrival of the guests.

Their reaction to her appearance gave Jenna food for thought: something very like chagrin showed in Carla's eyes, while Alex made no attempt to hide his admiration, coming forward to hand her a glass of sherry and whisper a compliment in her ear.

Soon the guests began to arrive, and Jenna and Carla were kept busy with introductions. The American girl recovered her poise and soon was the center of a lively, laughing group. When they went in to dinner, as guest of honour she was escorted by Ross, while Alex hastily appointed himself Jenna's escort.

Mrs. Frazer surpassed herself, providing a meal such as Jenna had never tasted before. Finally, there was much talk over brandy and chocolates but, even so, the moment came all too soon when they all rose and followed their host into the balcony room, where the grand piano stood invitingly open.

Ross led Jenna across to it, made sure the light was where she wanted it, nodded encouragingly to her and went back to where his guests were drinking coffee.

Jenna's heart was beating quickly as her fingers touched the cold keys, but as always with the first notes, her nervousness left her and she became absorbed in the music. Finishing her selection, her hands fell into her lap in an unconsciously graceful gesture, while behind her there were appreciative murmurs.

Alex brought her a cup of coffee. "That was great, Jenna," he said. "Come and join the others."

Ross looked up and smiled as she approached but said nothing before turning back to Carla. The conversation became general and Jenna found the other guests friendly as they included her easily in their talk. But suddenly she realized how the unaccustomed drink and excitement had made her head spin, and at the first opportunity, she slipped across the room and out onto the balcony, hoping she was unobserved.

After the warm room, thick with cigar smoke and the smell of coffee and brandy, the night air was fresh and slightly damp on her heated cheeks. Leaning against the cool stone wall, she lifted her face into the breeze, smelling the ozone and enjoying the wind in her hair. Behind her a shadow stepped into the pool of light from the window and, dismayed, she realized that someone had seen her leave.

"Are you all right, Miss Clair?" asked Ross Trent.

"A little tired, that's all," she answered hastily, thinking he would go back. But he came across to stand beside her.

"And your head aches."

"A . . . little," she agreed, wondering at his perception.

"Mrs. Frazer tells me that you helped her prepare for this evening. I gave you the day off so that you could rest."

"I enjoyed helping her. Do you mind?" she asked curiously.

"You may do what you like with your free time. I make no claim on you so long as your work is done to my satisfaction." He studied her somewhat chastened expression for a moment and then went on in a warmer tone. "My guests enjoyed your performance this evening."

"I'm glad," she said simply, and went on, with a hint of shyness in her voice. "May I thank you for this?" Her hand caressed the shimmering skirt of her dress.

"My pleasure," he said briefly. "I'm glad you like it."

She was unable to stop herself asking the question that had puzzled her all evening. "How did you—how does it . . . ?"

"I asked Mrs. Frazer to look in your wardrobe." His eyes gleamed at her and amusement sounded clearly in his voice. "My dear girl, did you think I'd sized you up?"

Biting her lip as the ready colour flooded her cheeks, she turned away saying stiffly, "Don't you think we had better go back to your other guests?"

Without a word, he held the curtain and stood back for her to enter. The room seemed much as she had left it. Pools of light cast a soft golden glow; people were deep in animated conversation; Alex was giving all his attention to a fair-haired girl and a young man. Only Carla looked up at their entrance, her eyes wide and cold as they met Jenna's across the room.

Six

As usual Carla failed to appear for breakfast and Jenna found the two brothers sitting at the table next morning. Murmuring a greeting, she slid into her seat and unfolded her napkin.

"Good morning, Miss Clair," smiled Ross Trent. "We hardly expected to see you this morning."

Jenna looked up from her grapefruit. "I thought that we'd be working as usual."

"You must think me a hard taskmaster. After you performed so admirably for us last night, the least I can do is give you the morning off."

"Good!" put in Alex. "I'll take her swimming—if that's all right, Jenna?"

Ross lifted his eyebrows at the use of her first name, but only advised them that the water would still be cold at this time of year.

After breakfast Jenna changed into a swimsuit and pulled trousers and a jumper on, before throwing a towel over her shoulder and running downstairs to join Alex, who was waiting in the hall.

The steps cut into the rock face were steep and difficult to negotiate, and she was glad when Alex took her hand. Pale wet sand stretched at their feet where the tide had recently receded from the foot of the cliff, leaving wickedly pointed rocks and knots of thick seaweed exposed. Dropping her clothes on a dry boulder, she dashed into the sea, followed by Alex. The coldness took away her breath and although she swam energetically for a few minutes, she was not sorry when her companion touched her wrist and motioned that they should return to the beach.

Teeth chattering, she rubbed herself vigorously and was thankful to feel the warmth of her dry clothes.

"Come on," urged Alex, taking in her shivering form, "a quick walk along the beach and you'll think it was worth it after all. At the moment you look like a frozen mermaid."

Jenna flicked drops at him from the ends of her wet hair and then shook it back from her face. Weighing their towels down with stones, they left them to dry and headed along the narrow strip of sand, each footstep leaving a clear-cut outline on the clean and pristine beach.

She was a country girl, born and brought up in a little Somerset village, and not since a childhood holiday had she known the delights of a walk beside the sea. Little pools had formed between the rocks, filled with clear water that was unexpectedly warm after the cold of the Atlantic. Small, pointed white shells showed clearly where the high water mark was and Jenna's pockets were soon filled with shells and stones of all colours.

The wind lifted her drying hair and, filled with well-being, she smiled at her companion. "This is lovely," she said.

"We must do it again," he agreed, placing one arm around her shoulders and tucking her against his side. They walked on in companionable silence for a while before he turned her around, remarking that it was time they returned to the castle.

Jenna looked back at the two lines of dark

footmarks leading around the point of the cliff and, for the first time, noticed Heron's Keep silhouetted against the blue sky. From this angle, it was grim and stark. All signs of luxury and modern living were hidden and she realized that it must have looked much the same for all the years since it was built.

"We could have slipped back in time," she said, repressing an involuntary shiver.

Following her gaze, he nodded, considering. "Yes—it would have looked about the same to the men who built it," he agreed. "Or to the Jacobites, hiding after the Rising."

"It's easy to see why they built it there—it's quite inaccessible from the sea."

"And the land—when the gates were closed and an army of men waited on the battlements. Heron's Keep may have changed hands once or twice, but it was never taken by force."

The girl looked up at the note of pride in his voice and was suddenly envious that he could lay claim to such a heritage. "Come on," she said, slipping out of his grasp and beginning to run along the beach. "I must wash my hair before lunch, and your brother won't be pleased if I present myself at the table wet and dripping."

Carla, who was lying on the terrace, opened her eyes as they closed the waterdoor behind them. Cool and eye-catching in white shorts and halter top, she raised a languid hand at their approach. "How energetic," she murmured.

"You should try it," advised Alex, sitting down beside her and peering into a pitcher that stood on a nearby table. "Mind if we have a drink?" he asked and, without waiting for her assent, poured out two glasses of squash.

"Sea water won't do your hair any good," said the

American girl, eyeing Jenna. "You look half drowned."

"Alex was kinder—he said a mermaid," murmured Jenna sipping her drink.

"Men are notoriously softer hearted than women." Carla stretched her long limbs and regarded the beginnings of a tan critically. "I'll wait until the weather's warmer before I make the effort—where I come from, we either swim in a heated pool or a warm sea. You both look half frozen and that's not my idea of enjoyment."

"The beach is interesting," offered the younger girl. "There are lots of shells and colourful stones down there."

Carla flicked an eye at the collection in the outstretched hand and touched them carelessly with a long fingernail. "Mmm—nice, but not really my kind of thing."

"Well—I'll go and wash my hair," Jenna said, standing up and putting her treasures back into her pocket, feeling rather chilled at the refusal of her tentative offer of friendship.

She washed the salt out of her hair and lay down on the bed with her head in a patch of sun, letting it dry in the warmth. Mentally she reviewed all that had happened in the last few days: she had found an easy camaraderie with Alex; knew there could never be more than an armed truce with Carla; while Ross Trent . . . was an enigma. Self-contained and arrogant, there was a surprising warmth about him at times—a kindness that he seemed to be ashamed of at other times, and hid under a cold manner. To say that she still disliked him would not be true: wary interest, with a tinge of apprehension, would better describe her feelings for him.

Sighing, she shook out her drying hair and followed the sunlight across the white bedspread.

She had been at Heron's Keep for several weeks now, and was no nearer solving the mystery of the inheritance or finding the lost 'Luck'.

Somehow, settling in and grasping the essentials of her job had taken all her thoughts and energy. But now that she was more used to the castle and its inmates she would give her mind to both factors. And, by coincidence, something happened that very afternoon: to her surprise, Ross was a major actor, though hardly in the role she had expected him to play.

They were in his study, he dictating some notes for her. Having reached the Seventeenth Century in his history of the keep, he was dealing with the help the Scots gave in the Civil War and battle of Worcester. One of the MacKenzies had been much involved, and Ross wanted to quote from one of his letters written after the battle. Failing to find it among the papers or Jenna's files, he bore her off to look for it.

"I remember there was quite a packet of them," he said, leading the way upstairs, "but I haven't seen them for years. My mother was interested in history and I know she had them at one time, so we'll start in her room."

Jenna followed him along a narrow corridor into one of the round towers. A few steps led up and around and stopped at a stout wooden door, black with age and studded with heavy square-head nails. Ross turned to look down at her, his hand on the brass ring that served as a handle and, reading her wide-eyed expression, allowed a smile to creep into his gaze.

"Not a dungeon, Miss Clair—nor am I Bluebeard, though you might be excused for thinking so, faced by so formidable a barrier as this." He ran his fingers over the old, grained wood and gave the ring a twist. As the door swung open, he said over his shoulder, "My mother restored this room to what it must have been when the castle was built. She found this door down in the cellars."

Jenna stood in the doorway and blinked as she took in the room before her. Dark paneling covered the octagonal walls, each of which was pierced by a narrow pointed window scarcely wider than an arrow slit. All the furniture was black and curved in the bulbous Tudor fashion. An ornate four-poster bed was hung with ancient, threadbare, embroidered curtains, while the walls were hung with small tapestries and pictures, darkened with the soot of centuries.

While she had no great liking for the Tudor age, she had to admit that the room was a masterpiece. Every item obviously had been chosen with great care to create just the right impression.

"It's—very impressive," she ventured at last.

"But not to your liking?"

"I like the balcony room better," she agreed by implication, "but your mother did a marvellous job here. It must have taken her ages to find each piece. Surely they weren't all here in the castle?"

"Some were ... I know she found a few at auctions, and some she bought from friends. It was her ambition to have a room furnished in each style. This, the balcony room, and mine were as far as she got."

"What period is yours?" She was unable to resist asking.

"Victorian," he answered briefly and, going to a huge chest that stood against the foot of the bed, opened the lid. "Did you know that this is called a hope chest?" he asked, smiling across at her. "Each girl was given one during her childhood and spent the intervening years filling it with the products of her needle, hoping to have it full by the time she married."

"I thought that was an American custom."

"Ours first! I dare say their ancestors took it with them when they left for the New World."

"It's rather a nice idea," she said, fingering the heavy lid and peering inside to see the space for linen filled with boxes, and bundles of papers tied with string and ribbon and elastic bands.

"One lot at a time, and re-tie it as we go, I think," said Ross, dropping a bundle into her lap as she knelt on the floor. He drew up a chair and for a while there was silence, except for the rustle of paper as they searched for the letters they wanted.

At last the man gave an exclamation. "Here they are," he said, slipping the thick sheets into his pocket. "Let's put these back, and then we can get on with my notes."

Jenna sighed. "I'd just found a recipe for a 'white complexion' that looked fascinating."

"You can come up here another time," Ross promised as he began putting the papers away.

Standing up, Jenna rocked on her toes, trying to relieve the tingle of blood rushing back into her cramped feet. Idly she walked about the room, pausing to look at this, touch that—until a portrait above the canopy of the stone fireplace caught her attention. Against a background so dark as to be almost black, a man's head and shoulders stood out vividly. A vibrant blue doublet covered the broad shoulders and a small white ruff framed an arrogant chin. The artist had painted the red hair so naturally that it seemed to gleam with life, while cool grey eyes met hers with a hint of a question in their depths. . . . She would have known the man anywhere. Her startled exclamation made Ross glance up.

"Did—did your mother have it painted?"

He came to stand behind her, inspecting the painting critically. "No. It's quite genuine."

"But—it's the image of you!"

He shrugged. "Such things do happen."

"But how can it—?" She broke off, seeing from his expression that she was pressing the subject too much and that soon he would begin to wonder at her insistence. Even now he was looking at her strangely.

"My dear girl, even odder things happen. I have another portrait which I'll show you one day." And, ignoring her inquiring eyes, he deliberately changed the subject, leaving her with several questions unanswered as they left the Tudor room and went back to the study.

Jenna found it hard to concentrate and was glad when her employer gave an exasperated sigh and dismissed her until the next day. But not until that night when she was in bed could she give her attention to the mystery. Far into the night she listened to the rhythmic waves and pondered just how Ross Trent could resemble some remote ancestor of the MacKenzies, when as far as she knew he had not a drop of MacKenzie blood in his veins.

Seven

The mystery still puzzled her the next day, her employer's clean-cut features and dark red hair presenting themselves between her eyes and her work until she could bear it no longer and admitted silently that she could not concentrate on typing Ross's notes while the matter filled her mind with speculation.

With sudden resolution, she stood up and, ignoring the pile of notes, left the room and headed in the direction Ross had led her the day before. Her footsteps echoed on the stone stairs behind her as she hurried up the short flight of steps towards the Tudor room. She hesitated with her hand on the brass ring before opening the door and stepped quickly into the room, before she should lose her nerve.

The portrait over the fireplace seemed to stare at her with familiar grey eyes, and she almost expected it to lift its eyebrows in query. Going closer she gazed up at the painted face, studying the features; without the cracks and patina of age she could have sworn that it was painted yesterday and that Ross Trent had sat for the artist. Thinking that there might be some information on the back, she tentatively tried to lift it away from the wall, but found that it was firmly fastened down. With a frustrated sigh she turned away, her gaze brightening a little as it fell on the hope chest. Thinking that she might find some answer to the mystery there, she raised the heavy lid.

Recalling that she had examined much of the contents the day before, she discarded most of the papers and books, selecting only an ancient and tattered *History of the Clan MacKenzie* and an account book which, she thought from the date, might belong to Lady Silis. Retiring to a windowseat where the light was better, Jenna examined her finds, only to find to her disappointment that the history was written in Gaelic and that the account book was involved solely with the kitchen. She was about to return them to the chest, when her eye was caught by a familiar name in the crabbed handwriting of Lady Silis' cook.

Paid to Granny Ewen for the still room, 2s 6d.

Quickly she glanced over the succeeding pages and found the same name several times more. Raising her head, she gazed thoughtfully out of the narrow window, pondering the new puzzle.

"You have a propensity, Miss Clair, for never being where I expect you," observed a voice suddenly, making her jump and drop the books on her lap onto the floor.

Hastily retrieving them, Jenna looked at her employer with a heightened colour, "You did say I might come here," she defended herself.

"I've no objection to you exploring the castle, but it might be a good idea if you left a note saying where to find you."

"I'm sorry, did you want me?"

"I'm dealing with '45, when Rory MacKenzie was—'out'—with the prince, and I find I need to refresh my memory. There was a tale that Granny Ewen used to tell me—" He lifted his eyes at her startled exclamation, and paused interrogatively.

"It's just that she's mentioned in this book I was

looking at—well, it can't be her actually because it is dated 1850 to 1870."

"Let me see!" Following her finger, Ross read the entries she pointed out. "It will be one of her relatives," he said, closing the book and replacing it in the chest. "You'll find that a certain family has a talent for particular things. The Trents are farmers, the MacKenzies were soldiers—the Ewens are seers and white witches."

He spoke as though such things were an every day occurrence, and Jenna was intrigued that such a practical man could accept the occult with equanimity.

"Do you believe in witches?" she asked curiously.

He gazed at her thoughtfully before replying, "If you mean, do I believe in love potions or ill-wishing, then no, I don't, but every Highlander knows that some folk can see more than others. Every clachan* has someone with 'the sight' . . . and who am I to dispute it?"

Jenna was quiet on the way to the croft,** clutching her pencil and notebook as though holding on to reality. Realizing her feelings, Ross sent her amused glances, but said nothing until they arrived outside the tiny cottage.

"If you'd rather stay in the car?" he suggested.

Aware of his amusement, Jenna shook her head with determination. "I've never met a witch before," she said truthfully. "I'd never forgive myself if I missed the opportunity."

"I hope you are not disappointed," he said gravely and, turning, led the way across the short grass to the front door that stood open.

*A small village in the Highlands or west of Scotland.

**Small, encircled field or rented farm.

"Come away in—the pot's on the boil," said a voice from the dark interior and with a fast beating heart Jenna followed her employer under the low lintel.

At first she could see nothing, but then her eyes gradually grew accustomed to the dimness and she could make out a neat room with a table in the centre covered with a crisp, white cloth and set for tea. A small figure was bending over a range, filling a brown teapot from the kettle. She looked up suddenly and Jenna found herself gazing into the brightest blue eyes she had ever seen. A mass of soft, white curls and a pink hand-knitted jumper completed the picture of the least witch-like woman she could imagine and involuntarily she sent Ross an indignant glance, which he blandly ignored.

"Well, Janet?" he said, dropping a kiss on her cheek. "How are you keeping?"

"Well enough, Mr. Ross," she answered, pleased by his attention. "And this young lady, now, what is it she's looking for?"

"I don't think she's looking for anything. This is Miss Clair who's working for me, typing the history I'm putting together. Which is why I'm here, Janet. Do you remember that story you used to tell Alex and me about Rory MacKenzie and the leap he made?"

"I ken the story fine."

"Will you tell it again and let Miss Clair take it down in her notebook?"

Again Jenna was the recipient of a bright, shrewd gaze and then the old woman nodded, having apparently made up her mind.

"But first we'll have a wee cuppee—no doubt you'll still have a taste for my pancakes. You liked them fine when you were younger."

The old woman bustled about preparing tea. The table was already laid with a pretty blue and white tea set and now she brought out plates of cakes and drop scones before pouring the tea. "Now," she said when everything was to her satisfaction and both her guests were the possessors of a steaming cup. "Help yourselves—I like to see a good appetite, and while you're sampling my cooking I'll tell you the tale of Rory's leap.

"Rory MacKenzie was a fine, braw laddie," she began, settling herself in her chair. "Big and handsome, with a fine red head to himself. There was none the lassies liked better, but the time we're talking of, he was a married man with a beautiful wife and a bonnie bairn to his name.

"He was a younger son and, while his brother stayed at home, he went off to join the prince. That way they'd have a foot in both camps, so to speak, and what ever happened, Heron's Keep would be safe for the family. Canny old folk, those Highlanders were. Well, Rory went off and fought bravely for the Jacobite cause. He was at Culloden and after the defeat he made his way home with the Redcoats hard on his heels. They knew fine he was there in front of them, but never a glimpse did they catch of him, for he knew these hills as well as the deer that roamed free. He led them a fine old dance, until he came to a ravine with a deathly drop to the river below and there he waited until the soldiers came up and himself clearly in sight. Then he took a good run at it and with a great jump he was across and safe on the other side, with none daring to follow. And he was away and aboard a vessel for France before the soldier boys even found their way to a road."

The soft voice transplanted Jenna back in time. So vividly did she imagine Rory and the chasing

Redcoats that as the old woman's voice died away,
she was surprised to look up and find herself seated
at a table and not upon some wild and windswept
mountainside. She looked across the cups and
plates and lifted her chin unconsciously, thinking
proudly that the story was about *her* ancestor.

Ross watched her, amused by her reaction. "Miss
Clair enjoyed your tale, Janet," he said, "for all she
should be on the side of the Redcoats."

The woman looked at him thoughtfully. "Miss
Clair is as much a Highlander as you, Ross Trent,"
she announced calmly, "for all she was born in
England. You'll find what you are looking for,
lassie—and more besides," she went on, and Jenna
saw that her eyes were blank and unseeing.

She would have said more, but Ross stood up and
said loudly that they must go. The old woman
started and looked around before, recovering herself, she smiled and allowed him to help her out of
her chair.

"That was interesting," commented Jenna as
they walked back to the car.

Her employer gave a noncommittal grunt and
busied himself opening the door. Jenna looked at
him curiously, wondering what had caused his
sudden change of mood—from calm good humour
to prickly irritation. After waving to the little figure
standing in the low doorway of the croft house as
they drove off, she did not gaze avidly out of the
window at the passing scene, but instead studied
her companion surreptitiously and thoughtfully.

"Don't stare," he said suddenly, his gaze on the
road ahead.

"For a moment there, I thought she was having
an attack of the second sight," said Jenna, giving
up all pretense and airing boldly the matter
which she suspected had provoked his ill temper.

71

Ross's hands tightened on the steering wheel until the knuckles showed white. Then with a visible effort he relaxed and loosened his grip.

"Janet Ewen saw my future once and what she told me didn't make pleasant hearing. I have no wish for anyone to have the same experience."

Although he spoke calmly, Jenna was aware of the controlled emotion behind his words.

"Is it to come—or has it happened?" she asked.

"Oh, it's happened all right!" he answered savagely. "And you see, I don't know whether Granny Ewen's prediction influenced me and my actions, and made it happen . . . or—"

"Whether it would have anyway," she finished for him.

"Exactly. So you see why I had no wish for another taste." Deliberately he changed the subject. "You seem very interested in Scottish history."

"I am," she answered. "That's why I took this job."

"It's strange that old Janet should say you were a Highlander," he went on slowly.

"My father always claimed Scottish blood a long way back," she told him, hoping that the half truth would satisfy his curiosity—which it apparently did, for he allowed the conversation to lapse and they were both busy with private thoughts during the remainder of the drive back to the castle.

"Ross, honey, where *have* you been?" Carla greeted them on their return. "Alex and I have hunted everywhere for you."

"We were out," he told her mildly.

Carla shot Jenna a quick glance before turning all her charm on Ross. "Well, now I've found you, you'll come with me, won't you?"

She hung onto his arm, pouting prettily up at him and Jenna felt a touch of chagrin as he responded to her appeal.

"Only tell me where," he said gallantly.

"Why, down to those dreadful old dungeons of yours Alex has been telling me about. I declare I was too scared to go with Alex here, but with you both to keep me company, I shall feel as safe as if I was with a troop of cavalry."

"How about you, Jenna?" asked Alex.

"Perhaps Miss Clair would prefer not to face another trip underground," suggested his brother.

"I'll look after you," Alex assured her with such an engaging smile that Jenna felt she could not disappoint him and agreed somewhat reluctantly.

With Ross and Carla in the lead, they set off into the bowels of the stronghold and, with Ross to point out the various features they passed, Jenna began to realize the age and strength of Heron's Keep.

Pausing beside a round grating set in the floor, Ross picked up a sliver of stone and dropped it between the iron bars. After an uncomfortably long time they heard a faint 'plop' from far below.

"The original well," he told them. "With a secure supply of water the castle was virtually impregnable. We still draw our water from it."

Carla was visibly disturbed. "I don't like to bother you, Ross, but you know I'm funny about things like that. Are you sure it's pure?"

"Better than any from a pipe," he assured her. "It was tested only a short while ago."

She eyed the dark hole doubtfully. "We-ll . . . I guess I can take your word for it. . . ."

"You can," he told her briefly.

"You Americans," teased Alex. "You'd much prefer treated water, filled with chemicals straight from a water plant, than our stuff, which has been cleaned by filtering down through the earth."

Carla shuddered. "Don't! It just doesn't seem clean to me."

"Well, you've drunk it ever since you arrived here with no ill effects," Ross reminded her and, sensing his impatience, the American girl abandoned her scruples.

"Don't think me difficult, Ross, honey," she pleaded, "it's just that I was brought up in an air-conditioned environment. In the States everything is cleaned and processed out of all recognition. I guess you'll just have to make allowances for little ole me."

She exaggerated her accent and fluttered her lashes as she gazed soulfully at him.

"You won't get around Ross that way," laughed his brother. "He's impervious to feminine wiles."

"Now, there you are mistaken," drawled the elder Trent. "I'll even collect some fresh water tablets especially for you, Carla, when next I go into town."

Carla was delighted. "For that, I'll drink your natural water and try not to think about it."

"Didn't you wonder why it was brown?" Alex asked mischievously.

"I—thought it was a chemical."

"It's the peat," Ross explained, shooting his brother a warning look. Taking Carla's arm, he hustled her along the corridor, firmly refusing to be drawn into further conversation on the subject.

"Now this," he said, stopping at a heavy wooden trapdoor in the stone floor, "is an oubliette."

Lifting the lid, he took a powerful torch from his pocket and shone it into the black depths. Jenna leaned forward to peer down and felt an arm close firmly around her waist.

"It's a long way down," said Alex quietly and, following the torch beam, she could see how true his words were.

A long narrow tunnel stretched downwards for about twenty feet, widening out a little at the bottom to a rough, rocky floor. About halfway down, a tiny slit in the wall let in a dim sliver of diffused light; everything was dank and green with mold and mildew. An involuntary shiver slipped down her spine and she shrank away from the loathsome sight, grateful to feel Alex's presence at her back.

"Ugh, what a horrid place!" she breathed.

"What is it?" Carla asked, peering down with excited interest.

"What every castle should have! Even in England I believe every stronghold was provided with one—oubliette means 'to forget'—a safe and secure prison where captives could be kept with no possible means of escape. If the prisoner was particularly disliked, then—we've all heard the expression 'thrown into a dungeon!'"

His words called up such a vivid picture to Jenna that she exclaimed in horror and hastily stepped back, all her previous claustrophobia brought to the fore.

"Well—fancy that!" came Carla's calm tones. "These old lords of yours sure were uncivilized."

Leaning against a rough wall, Jenna glanced up unhappily at the low ceiling, trying to conceal the apprehension she was feeling. Sensing eyes upon her, she looked around to meet Ross's grey gaze.

"Shall we go up?" he suggested, dropping the trapdoor in place. "I believe Miss Clair doesn't like it down here."

"Oh, Ross," pouted Carla. "I was just getting interested. Didn't Alex say there are some proper cells, with chains and things?"

"We've been here rather a long time. Mrs. Frazer will think we're lost."

"It won't take long, and now we're here it seems a pity not to see what we came for."

Trying to hide the shivers that shook her, Jenna felt obliged to offer to go on.

"Why not go back by yourself, hon?" suggested the other girl. "All the lights are on so you won't miss the way."

"You take Carla on, Alex," said Ross, "while I go back with Miss Clair."

Alex shook his head. "You're the one for history lessons, big brother," he told him. "I've had enough of this place myself. Jenna and I'll see you upstairs."

The journey back was taken at a quick pace, but even so she was inordinately relieved to see the light of day and feel the wind on her face as Alex led her out onto the terrace.

"I don't care for the depths myself," he told her, putting a glass of wine into her hand.

Jenna sipped gratefully. "I had no idea that the old chieftains were so fierce—or life so hard," she said slowly.

"It wasn't all romantic. Heron's Keep has many a story and mystery which no one will ever know."

She looked at him quickly, half wondering if he was hinting at the reason behind her being there. But his guileless expression convinced her that there was no ulterior motive behind his words. Sighing she looked away, staring out to sea, feeling guilty at her own subterfuge and evasions; Alex was such a nice person that she hated deceiving him. While admitting that she did not have the same reservations about his brother, who appeared remote and formidable enough to take care of himself, she knew uneasily that even towards Ross, her feelings were changing.

Why, I might even find myself liking you, Ross Trent. The thought was unexpected, and the sudden realization filled her with surprise and something very like excitement.

Eight

"Come and meet Euan," said Alex, as Jenna paused on the stairs, unwilling to disturb him as he seemed deep in conversation with a man she had not seen before. "Miss Clair meet Euan MacKenzie, Ross's farm manager. He's just back from three months' furlough visiting his brother in Australia."

"How do you do, Miss Clair," said the overseer, and Jenna found herself being appraised by a pair of shrewd light blue eyes. "No doubt you're finding it strange here after your southern ways."

"Not really—I like it here very much. How was Australia?"

"Interesting . . . but not for me. I like my grass to be green and Scottish."

"I can understand how you feel," the girl smiled, and won a softened expression from the somewhat stern man before her. With his pale eyes and light-coloured hair, he was every Englishman's idea of a Scot and he certainly seemed to live up to the reputation of being dour.

"Does he live in the castle, too?" she asked when Euan had left.

"Good heavens no! Euan would never put up with that—he's one who likes his independence. He has a little house in the village and seems to look after himself quite well."

"I mean he has the name of MacKenzie."

"I see you haven't much idea of our clan system. We all share the name, but still have different families and classes, although we live in the same area."

"But—you're not a MacKenzie!" she asked, puzzled.

"MacKenzie-Trent, by rights a double barrel, but we don't use it much."

"When did you adopt it?"

"Sometime in the last century," he answered indifferently, apparently not noticing her confusion for he went on quickly, "look here, sorry to dash off, but I promised Carla I'd take her into town and I'm late already. She'll never forgive me if I keep her waiting any longer."

Jenna watched his flying figure as he ran across the hall and took the steps down to the courtyard two at a time. Dimly she heard a car start, before she turned away, puzzling over what Alex had just told her. She seemed to be surrounded by mysteries at every turn, she thought wryly, shrugging impatiently. The Trents had probably taken the name as a sop to local feeling and loyalty, she decided, and continued her interrupted walk to her workroom.

Carla and Alex were not back for dinner and, as Ross had his on a tray in his study where he was closeted with his factor, Jenna ate her meal in solitude. Afterwards, she wandered into the balcony room, running her fingers along the keys of the piano as she stared out of the open window across the sea which was still bright, but misty with approaching evening. Impulsively, she ran upstairs, changed into trousers and a thin jumper before, letting herself out of the watergate, she climbed down the stone steps to the beach below.

Wandering contentedly over the damp sand, her pockets and hands soon filled with new treasures, she did not realize how dark it had become, or how quickly the tide had come in. Suddenly aware of her surroundings, she looked back in time to see the first wave touch the bottom of the steps in the cliff—and knew, with a sinking heart, that she could never reach them before they were covered by water.

The wind had freshened with the turning tide and now blew in from the sea, making the waves, that had seemed small and playful so short a while ago, rough and fierce. Water splashed at her feet, sucking the ground away with its undertow, and she stepped back hastily, wrapping her arms around her chilled body.

With a growing fear, Jenna looked about. Ahead, the sea was racing to fill the loch and already the stretch of sand that she stood on was perceptibly smaller than minutes ago. Her only hope seemed to be the rocks and boulders that surrounded the base of the cliff on which Heron's Keep stood, and with a shiver of fright she realized that even they might be covered at high tide.

By the time she reached the rocks and had clambered up to their illusory shelter, the light had gone from the evening sky and, in the growing darkness, she felt very alone and vulnerable.

Perched on the rounded top of a boulder, Jenna sniffed dolefully as the hungry waves began to lap at her refuge. A tear trickled slowly down her cheek to join the salt of the sea spray and she brushed it away impatiently as she searched the cliff face behind her for hand and toe holds.

"Halloa . . . Jenna, are you there?"

At Ross Trent's voice above her, she raised her head with new hope—but could see nothing in the blanketing darkness. "Yes, oh yes, down here!" she answered eagerly.

"Stay there—you'll be all right for a moment."

Jenna never doubted the authority in his voice

and, only conscious of relief that she was saved, leaned against the rock behind her. Soon, sounds of movement and little chippings falling past her told her that someone was climbing down the face of the cliff. Aware of that steep and precipice-like wall, she realized the danger involved and a new fear came to her. Hiding her face in her hands she crouched against the rock, waiting to hear the sickening sound of a body falling. In her misery, she was unaware that the sounds of climbing had ceased—until a hand touched her shoulder.

"Praying, Miss Clair?" asked her employer.

"You might have been killed," she gasped, looking up.

"Nonsense. Alex and I often came down that way as boys," the man said bracingly. Taking her arm, he pulled her to her feet before she could point out that that must have been several years ago. "We'll have to move quickly," he said, "these rocks will be covered soon."

With a hand gripping her above the elbow, he guided her over the rocks, lifting, pushing, encouraging, until she was breathless and dizzy, half-blinded by spray, and quite lost.

Suddenly she was dragged into an interior even darker than the night outside. A door was thrust closed and the roar of the elements dropped to a murmur.

"Where—where are we?" she gasped, clinging to his arm as the only stable element in an unknown world.

"In an old fisherman's croft—you're quite safe. The sea never comes as high as this."

His voice was curt and, as he put her hand away and moved out of reach, Jenna was only too aware of the air of anger about him. A match flared and in its light she saw him busy with an oil lamp that hung from the roof. Then the wick caught and the tiny room was bathed in a golden glow that barely touched the corners filled with shadows. A workbench filled one wall, with a small rowing dinghy taking up most of the floor space, while a camp bed standing under the single small window seemed to be the sole item of furniture.

Jenna became aware of Ross's angry eyes on her and, guiltily aware of her carelessness in taking a walk along the beach without first checking the tide, she shuffled her feet like a child waiting for a scold.

"Of all the imbeciles!" her employer exploded, and she knew that he had kept his temper in check until they had reached safety. "Competent and sensible were my requirements for a secretary, Miss Clair—and you are obviously neither. Of all the stupid, irresponsible things to do! Do you realize you might easily have been drowned?"

She did realize it only too well and, hanging her head to hide her tears from his cold eyes, she shivered desolately.

"I . . . like the beach, and the time went more quickly than I realized," she defended herself inadequately.

"Indeed? Well, next time I might not be around to rescue you. If Mrs. Frazer hadn't seen you and told me—" He broke off, looking at her more closely as she shuddered at the picture his words conjured up. His fingers touched her cheek, then her hand, and he said more kindly, "You're frozen and I suppose your shoes are wet. Sit on the bed and take them off while I see if I can find something to dry you."

The laces of her shoes were knotted hard with sea water and defied her attempts to untie them. Ross returned with a towel and, seeing her fumbling fingers, knelt suddenly in front of her and quickly performed the task. Then, peeling off her sodden socks, he briskly dried her feet, rubbing until warmth returned.

"Dry your hair," he commanded, dropping the towel into her lap while he swung her legs around and up onto the camp bed, tucking a nylon windbreaker about her. "Not so good as a blanket, but it's all that's down here," he said. "It's lucky that Alex and I use this cottage as a boating house or there'd be nothing here at all. As it is, we've a little spirit stove and several tins of soup—we won't starve before morning."

She looked up at him, her eyes dark and startled in her pale face. "We've got to stay here all night?"

He nodded, a glimmer of amusement on his stern face. "Afraid so—or at least until the tide goes down."

"But we can't! What will people say?"

"You should have thought of that before you went for your walk."

"I hardly knew that you were going to follow me," said Jenna crossly.

"If I hadn't, my dear girl, you would hardly be in a position now to worry about my seducing you."

She gasped at his effrontery and looked up to meet his amused gaze. Then, lowering her own wrathful eyes, she huddled further into her nest of sailing clothes.

"You look like a seal woman or a naiad," he said outrageously and, taking a long lock of hair in his fingers, he tugged it gently. "Will you slip away to join your seafolk before morning?"

"How would you explain my absence if I did?"

He released her hair. "I'd say I didn't find you," he answered simply, standing up and taking a bottle from a shelf above their heads. "I've just remembered there's some brandy here—have some, it'll warm you."

Jenna hesitated, but the cold still creeping through her bones defeated any scruples she felt and obediently she raised the bottle. A hand ruthlessly tilted it further and she spluttered as the fiery spirits burned her throat.

"It will do you good," said Ross blandly, meeting her indignant eyes before he busied himself at the table, pumping up the stove as the soup heated and then pouring it into two huge mugs. "Not as good as Mrs. Frazer's," he said, handing one to Jenna, "but it will serve its purpose."

"Do the others know we're here?" she asked, cupping the mug in her chilled hands and sipping the steaming liquid.

"Alex and Carla were still out. Mrs. Frazer does, of course."

She sighed involuntarily, thinking how much she'd sooner have had Alex be the brother to rescue her.

"You'll have to put up with me."

She looked up quickly, surprised that he showed so much perception. "I—didn't mean to be rude," she apologized, "but he's—not so intimidating."

He raised an eyebrow, making her flounder into more explanations and watching as her discomfiture grew.

"Not that you—I mean you *are* rather remote while Alex is kind." The silence between them grew. "Oh dear . . . I didn't mean that you are not. Just that you seem rather cold and indifferent . . . sometimes."

"Shall we leave it at that, Miss Clair?"

The ice in his voice brought Jenna to a halt as nothing else could have done. She bit her lip, flushing uncomfortably as he stood up and, taking the mugs with him, went outside. The howling wind rose momentarily as he opened the door and sank to a murmur again when he closed it behind him.

When he returned he glanced briefly across the room at her, his rather dour expression relaxing a little at the sight of her forlorn figure huddled in the cocoon of green nylon.

"We'll have to share," he said, pulling a nylon sail from a locker. Sitting beside the girl, he spread it over them both. "Come closer," he advised, "and we'll keep each other warm."

"I'm quite warm enough," Jenna said stiffly—and untruthfully.

"Well, I'm not," said her companion, pulling her against him and putting his arm firmly around her. "Stay still," he commanded as she stiffened at his touch and tried to pull away. His breath warmed her cheek and although she wouldn't raise her eyes she knew he was looking down at her, and she could picture the amusement his eyes held. "Count it as a necessity . . . as something that has to be borne—and the time will soon go."

Jenna relaxed slowly as she felt sleep overcoming her, unwilling to admit even to herself that she liked the feel of his hard arm about her, that his nearness was strangely comforting—and that she felt more secure in the little sea-bound cottage than she had ever felt before.

Nine

She awoke to a bright glare of sunlight piercing the narrow window like a cinema spotlight. For a moment she lay still, trying to recognize her surroundings, and then a movement beside her drew her startled attention and she stared in amazement at her unexpected companion. Seconds later, her memory of the previous night's events returned, she drew away, trying to slip out of the close embrace of Ross Trent's arms. His grip tightened and she knew that he was awake.

"Good morning, Mr. Trent," she said, with a tolerable attempt at composure.

Grey eyes opened and met hers. "Awake at last?" he said calmly. "You're quite a slug-a-bed, my girl."

"I had a trying evening," she pointed out reasonably, sitting up. For a moment she thought he was reluctant to release her, then his arms fell away and he stretched his body. "I—I didn't thank you for coming to my aid last night," she said slowly.

He looked at her. "I thought you did." He grinned suddenly. "I could hardly have left you to drown—no matter how cold and remote I may be."

Jenna dropped her eyes. "I'm sorry about that," she murmured.

"Let's say you were under stress at the time."

"I wouldn't have said it otherwise—"

"No matter how much you meant it."

Her eyes flew to his, trying to read his expression, then the corners of her mouth trembled and suddenly they were both laughing.

He stood up, untangled the sailcloth coverings from about their legs and then pulled her to her feet.

"A truce, Miss Clair," he suggested, holding her hand.

"That would be a good idea," she agreed demurely, feeling the warmth of his fingers. Momentarily his grip tightened, then he let her go.

"Take my jacket," he said, shrugging out of the garment.

"But you? You'll be cold."

"I'll wear a sailing jacket. Now don't offer to take it yourself—you'd be lost inside it."

He pulled open the door and light filtered into the gloomy interior. A blast of fresh, ozone-laden air made Jenna breathe appreciatively and she went to stand beside him, looking past his shoulder.

Without turning, he put his arm about her, drawing her in front of him. "Rather different from last night."

She looked at the thin line of silver sea, calm and flat as it edged the smooth, almost colourless sand; the sky, clear and pale, until it fell into violet mist at the edge of the surrounding mountains.

"It's beautiful," she breathed.

"Aye—there's nowhere like it," Ross Trent agreed and, for the first time, she heard the Highland lilt in his voice. Suddenly she realized that her employer was not so English as he seemed.

"We'd best away—if we hurry, you can have a few hours in bed before breakfast." Taking her hand, he set off across the sand with a long purposeful stride that covered the ground quickly.

They parted at the foot of the stairs in the hall. "I'll

ask Mrs. Frazer to bring your breakfast up to your room," he said. "I'll not ask you to work this morning . . . doubtless you could do with a rest."

As he turned and walked quickly away his lithe step told Jenna that he needed no such consideration himself, and she determined to follow his example. But when she arrived in her room and saw the inviting bed, she forgot her resolutions and, falling into its ample depths, was soon sound asleep.

Mrs. Frazer's entry some time later aroused her and she saw by the bedside clock that it was past nine.

"Mr. Ross said to let you sleep on," said the housekeeper following her eyes. "That was a foolish thing to do, Miss Clair, if you don't mind me saying so."

"I know, Mrs. Frazer. I've already been told so."

"Ah well, Mr. Ross always did have a sharp tongue in his head—but it goes with a kind heart." She settled a tray on the girl's knees and smiled as Jenna eagerly attacked the food before her. "The others are getting up a party to the Highland Games being held near the town and Mr. Ross wondered if you'd care to go with them?"

"I'd love to, but isn't there any work for me to do?"

"As he made the offer, I should think not. What shall I say, Miss?"

"Please tell him that I should like it very much."

"I believe they are leaving about eleven, so there's no need to hurry."

But when Jenna came downstairs she found both men waiting in the hall. A shaft of sunlight touched her employer's red head and she was struck by how well he suited his surroundings; with dark paneling and bright weapons as background, he could have been a Highland Gentleman from any century.

"Am I late? I'm sorry if I've kept you waiting."

"Carla's still to come," said Alex, stepping forward. "Ross has been telling me about your adventure."

"I'm afraid I was rather silly—"

"He told me you were very brave."

Her eyes darted across to the older brother. Meeting her surprised gaze he smiled fleetingly as he turned on his heel, saying he was going to put the hamper in the car.

"It's a good thing we still use the old crofter's cottage and keep a few things there," Alex went on, "or you would have spent a very cold night."

Jenna felt a blush burning in her cheeks as she remembered Ross's arms about her and looked uneasily away from Alex's suddenly inquiring eyes.

"I'd take my oath that Ross was the soul of propriety, Jenna—surely he didn't make a pass at you?"

"No—of course not. It's just that . . . well, we had to keep each other warm."

His laughter filled the hall. "And I've never thought my brother one for assignations."

Carla paused on the last step, frowning at his words as she glanced from him to Jenna. Although her eyes narrowed at the girl's telltale flushed cheeks, she said nothing, but swept by her with raised eyebrows and a cloud of perfume.

"Alex, honey, have I kept you waiting?" she asked, taking his arm possessively.

Over her head, Alex shot Jenna a speaking glance before obediently leading the way out to the car. Ross was on the raised walk, leaning on the parapet as he gazed out to sea, but at their approach, he came down the steps to hold the door for the girls. Carla took the seat beside the driver as though by right, leaving the back seats for Jenna and Alex.

The big, luxurious car slid smoothly out of the castle yard, taking the hill easily and purring along the narrow, winding road that led between impressive mountains and rock-strewn valleys. Jenna was pleased to be able to sit back and admire the scenery; the last time she had driven this way, she had had to concentrate on the tortuous road and her forthcoming interview with her new employer.

Jenna knew that Carla and Ross were holding an animated conversation, but she was content to lean back and gaze at the points of interest as Alex indicated them. Almost too soon, it seemed to her, they reached their destination. Ross paid some money, swept under a flag-decked archway and found a space to park the car on the mountainside opposite.

"Time for lunch," he said, "and then we'll go and find some seats at the ringside."

"There doesn't seem to be much happening," observed Carla, a note of disparagement in her voice.

"Everything stops for food," Alex explained. "We're a nation who take our meals seriously."

"True—who's going to open the basket and set it out?" Ross looked inquiringly from Jenna to Carla.

Carla waved a hand languidly. "Let Miss Clair. I'm sure she would do it beautifully. She's so competent . . . I should be useless."

Jenna's dark eyes sparked at Carla's arrogance and she was only slightly mollified at Ross's words:

"Please do, Miss Clair. We'd be very grateful."

Giving in with grace, she smiled at him and swung her slim legs to the ground. "Shall we have it outside? It's a lovely day."

Alex opened the trunk and, extracting the wicker hamper, carried it around the side of the car and placed it on the grass at her feet. She found a neat red and white checked cloth inside and she spread it on the ground. Then she fell to examining the food packed in plastic containers, feeling that even the redoubtable Mrs. Frazer had surpassed herself.

"Let's go and find seats," said Ross, when they had eaten. "The people are beginning to arrive."

Immediately Carla was on her feet, slipping her hand into the crook of his elbow. "I feel quite excited. Back home in the States there's nothing I like better than a rodeo."

"Our games are hardly that. We go in more for dancing, tossing the caber and that sort of thing," said Ross dryly, yet Jenna noticed that he didn't remove Carla's possessive hand but covered it with his own as they moved away.

"Shall we go?"

She started at the touch of Alex's hand on her shoulder and hoped her interest in his brother had not been too obvious. "I've never been to Highland Games before," she said quickly to hide her confusion. "Shall I enjoy them?"

"I hope so. Of course ours are small and nothing like the ones the Royal family goes to, but we enjoy ourselves. This evening, if the weather's fine, they'll lay boards on the arena and have dancing."

"Dancing?"

"Nothing sophisticated, I'm afraid. Flings and country dances."

"It sounds fun," she said truthfully and earned an appreciative smile from her companion.

In fact, Jenna enjoyed everything very much, seeming to find an affinity with the Highland folk who lined the sides of the ring. Cheering on the contestants as though she had done it all her life, she delighted in the display of dancing and felt an awakening thrill at the wild yells and fierce shouts that accompanied the flying feet.

As the ring emptied for the last time she sank back in her seat exhausted and contented. Feeling eyes upon her, she turned to meet Ross's grey gaze and smiled happily at him.

"You did that to the mannerborn," he commented.

"I enjoyed it."

"So I could see." He stood for a moment, towering over her, his expression more kindly than she had ever seen before. Then Carla touched his arm and he turned away.

"Let's find refreshments of some kind, Ross honey," the American girl begged charmingly.

"I'm sure we'd all like that," he said, and waited until Jenna and Alex had collected their belongings before leading the way into a huge tent that had been erected near the entrance.

When they came out, the scene had been transformed by a team of willing workers. The trodden grass of the arena was covered by wooden boards laid close together and forming a smooth floor. Coloured lights that hung from the encircling poles made bright pools in the gathering dusk. Jenna was glad that she had resisted the temptation to wear trousers, knowing that her smoky blue dress with its simple lines and easy skirt became her and was just right for the evening's entertainment before them.

A group of young men in jeans and tartan shirts took over a raised platform and soon the loudspeakers were giving out lively music with a well-marked beat.

"Shall we dance?" asked Alex, and Jenna saw that Carla and Ross were already on the floor.

"I—don't know how."

"You'll soon find out nothing could be easier." His hand between her shoulder blades propelled her firmly onto the floor where he seized her hands and swung her into a gay rhythm.

Jenna soon found, to her relief, that he was right. The dance was easy to pick up and soon she stopped worrying about where her feet or her partner were going and gave herself up to pure enjoyment.

Alex introduced her to several friends in the

milling throng and she found herself claimed for every dance. Ross and Carla seemed to dance exclusively with each other. Sometimes she caught a glimpse of their red and blonde heads close together and knew a strange pang of emotion that she was reluctant to admit was jealousy.

She had just taken part in a particularly energetic 'Dashing White Sergeant' and was returning to her seat, flushed and breathless, when a hand on her arm detained her.

"May I have the next dance?" Ross asked.

"Well . . . I'm rather tired. I was just going to sit down," she stammered, remembering the fact that he had ignored her all evening.

Releasing her, he stepped back as the music started.

"Oh . . . it's a waltz!" she exclaimed involuntarily.

"I take it that a waltz is different," her companion said dryly, taking her in his arms.

"They are usually slower," she pointed out.

"You'll find ours are different. We favour the old-fashioned kind." And before she could say anything he swept her into the dance.

Around and around, dipping in time to the insistent music he led her, his hand warm and firm just above her waist giving her the strangest feeling of being a prisoner. Only too aware of his hard body close against hers, Jenna kept her eyes obstinately lowered.

"Do you approve of my tie?" he asked at last.

She raised her eyes fleetingly to his face. "As it happens, I do—but my opinions scarcely matter, do they?" Lowering her head, she bit her lips and wondered why the remark had been jolted out of her.

"Tired, Miss Clair?" her partner asked solicitously. "Perhaps the day has been too long for you after the excursions of last night."

Jenna missed her step and his grip tightened quickly until she had regained her balance. "Oh, you're impossible!" she exclaimed. Then realizing the rudeness of her remark, she quickly apologized.

Ross's hand tilted her chin and his cool grey eyes examined her face, noting the dark shadows under her eyes that gave her a rather beguiling air of fragility. "I should be the one to say I'm sorry," he said with a rare contrite note in his voice. "I was teasing you—"

He gathered her closer, his arms holding her with a new gentleness. Her head dropped until her cheek rested against his shoulder, her dark lashes fluttering as she fought an almost overwhelming desire for sleep.

"Home for you, my sweet," he said into her ear as he caught his brother's eye and gestured that it was time they left.

Despite Carla's half-hearted protests, they were soon in the car heading towards Heron's Keep. Before the purring engine lulled her to sleep, Jenna wondered drowsily if she had really heard Ross give her an endearment. Watching with heavy eyelids as he bent his head towards the American girl and laughed at something she had said, she doubted the evidence of her ears and knew a momentary disappointment before her eyes closed.

Ten

Jenna typed Ross's notes steadily through the next morning, rather pleasantly conscious of her own virtue when she did not even stop for coffee. A little later, just as she was feeding a sandwich of paper and carbon into her machine, the door opened and her employer appeared.

"We wondered where you were," he commented.

"I thought I'd work straight through this morning," she explained as he perched on the corner of her desk, one long leg swinging. She typed a line with brisk efficiency and was chagrined to see that her fingers had missed the right keys.

"Really, Miss Clair," murmured Ross Trent, amused. "I hope the rest of your typing's better than that."

Nibbling her lips in annoyance, Jenna ripped the paper from the roller, but before she could replace it with fresh sheets, fingers closed over her wrist. For a moment she was motionless under his grip. Then she raised her eyes to his face, hoping her expression would not betray the tumult of her feelings.

"I've something else planned for this morning," he said easily. "I thought we could go to the attics and search out a few things to have photographed. They tell me that publishers like a book to be illustrated."

"That—sounds exciting."

"Could be—though Carla didn't think so."

Following his tall back out of the room, Jenna noted that he had obviously asked the American girl to accompany him first, and some of her pleasure at the prospect of exploring the attics evaporated. Even the thought that she might find some clue to the 'Luck' scarcely raised her spirits.

Ross led the way up the winding stone staircase, past the Tudor room with the portrait so like himself, and around and around until Jenna was reminded of the dance of the evening before.

"Now I know why you're so fond of the old-fashioned waltz," she panted, and he looked down at her and laughed but didn't slow his long stride until they reached a wide landing with several doors leading off.

"These were servants' quarters," he explained, opening a door and walking into a wide low room.

As Jenna joined him, a cloud obscured the sun and in an instant the room became dark and unwelcoming. She gazed out of a window that seemed unnaturally low—its sill starting only a few inches from the floor—and shivered involuntarily.

"What a cold room. I—don't like it much," she whispered, clasping her arms about herself and looking around.

Ross looked at her strangely. "Why not?"

She shook her head. "I don't know," she said honestly.

"Let's go into one of the others," he suggested sensibly. "This one seems empty anyway—we'll find nothing here."

Jenna was only too willing and by the time they had crossed the landing and entered another room, the sun had come out again and her feeling of depression had vanished.

"Do you have the sight?" Ross asked abruptly, his

back to her as he opened a glass-fronted cupboard.

"No . . . at least I don't know. If you mean second sight, I've never thought about it. Why?"

Taking out some china figures, he turned to look at her. "The attics are supposed to be haunted," he said intent upon the ornaments, "but I've always suspected that the story is there because no self-respecting castle is complete without a ghost."

"I don't think I really believe in ghosts," said the girl stoutly, privately suspecting that it would be a different matter if she was without his comforting presence.

"Good," he said approvingly. "Let's set to work."

Soon the table in the middle of the room was dusted and several possible subjects for illustrations placed upon it. Ross had moved into still another room when Jenna opened a chest and gasped in delight as her hands felt among soft folds of velvet and smooth silk.

"I've found some dresses," she called excitedly. "May I take them out?"

Ross appeared in the doorway. "If you're careful. I expect some are fragile."

Almost reverently she lifted out the dresses and laid them gently on a convenient row of chairs. A Regency muslin followed the heavy folds of a panniered brocade, and then her hands drew out a shimmering gown of rose silk. From a tiny waist the skirt burst out like a full-blown rose, and huge puffed sleeves fell away from the low curved neckline.

"It's as fresh as the day it was put away," she said, standing up and holding the dress against her.

Suddenly aware of a growing silence, she glanced up to find Ross looking fixedly at her, a strange expression on his face. For a moment their eyes held, hers puzzled and questioning, his rather bleak and suddenly shuttered.

"That might make a good photo," he said into the silence, and she had the oddest idea that it was not what he was thinking. "Perhaps you'd wear it; it wouldn't fit Carla."

"I'd love to," said the girl, impulsively laying her cheek against the cool folds of silk and, for a moment, an elusive perfume rose from the old dress, filling her nostrils with a timeless scent.

"Bring it down with you," commanded her employer and, turning away, he would have left the room but for a sudden exclamation from Jenna that made him stop on the threshold. "What is it?"

"There's a box in the bottom of the chest."

"Well there's nothing so strange about that." He reached a long arm in and took out a small inlaid wooden box. Jenna's heart seemed to stand still as he opened it, but it was empty, filled only with the smell of the sandalwood from which it was made.

"Why did you cry out?" he asked curiously, turning it over in his hands.

She shook her head. "I don't know," she said lamely. "It looked like an animal or something . . . a rat perhaps."

"Bring the dress and come down," he directed again and left the room, taking the box with him.

Jenna stared after him. How could she tell him that she had recognized the box as twin to one that had belonged to her family? One that by tradition had belonged to the Lady Silis and was called the 'Luck Box', a name that suddenly seemed full of unsuspected meaning.

When she arrived downstairs, she found Ross examining his spoils in his workroom. But of the box there was no sign. He looked up at her question, his brows raised a little.

"I've put it in my room," he said, not bothering to hide the fact that he wondered at her query as he studied her for a moment before returning to his work.

She hesitated by the door and at last he looked up again, a shade impatiently. "Is there something you want?"

And she found herself asking a question that had bothered her for some time. "I was only wondering— you'll think me very curious. You have an overseer so you must have a farm—but where is it?"

Relaxing, he smiled. "Not a farm in the English sense of the word. I have forests, and a herd of Highland cattle that I breed from and sell abroad. It's surprising how many foreign countries are interested in our beasts."

"I see," she said slowly.

"Would you like to see them sometime?"

"The trees or the beasts?"

"Both, if you're interested."

"I would like that very much."

"We'll arrange it someday then." He turned back to his papers and, feeling herself dismissed, she opened the door—but his voice stopped her in the entrance.

"You may have the rest of the day to yourself once you've finished my notes." He looked at her curiously. "What will you do?" he asked.

"I wondered about going to Glen Clair."

"Why not? It's a beautiful place . . . and your namesake."

"Is it easy to find?"

"None easier. Take the left turning just the other side of the hill beyond the castle."

He returned to his work and Jenna left the room to continue typing, determined to finish her work in good time so as to have most of the afternoon to explore Glen Clair.

Later, it was with a flutter of excitement that she started her car and set off along the road to her destination. Once she had left the narrow major road and turned onto the even narrower track Ross had described, she found herself between two high, brown mountains whose air of antiquity filled her with awe and a feeling of insignificance. The layered rock had fallen in places and lay in piles rather like cairns beside the winding road. Everywhere were sheep, their bleating filling the air with perpetual soft sound.

At last she came in sight of a small loch and followed its undulating shore until she found the ruins of a tiny croft at the far end. Stopping her car where the road ended in a pile of shingle, she rested her hands on the wheel and looked about.

Winding down the window, she studied her surroundings. The air was warm and heavy, filled with the somnolence of late afternoon. The wind ruffled her hair, carrying with it the sweet smell of heather and, high overhead in the clear blue sky, a lark trilled lazily.

Jenna opened the car door and climbed out, a feeling of well-being contentment growing within her. Wandering slowly towards the croft she disturbed two lambs that had been curled together behind a boulder and, bleating indignantly, they ran away in search of their mother.

The windows and door of the croft had long since vanished but the walls and roof were still reasonably sound and, after hesitating for a while, she stepped over the flagstoned doorway into the dark interior. For a moment she could see nothing, then gradually her eyes grew accustomed to the dim light and she could make out her surroundings. A huge fireplace filled one wall and, walking into its depths, Jenna could look up and see a square of sky at the top of the black chimney. On the opposite side of the room was the remains of what could only be a wall bed, its cupboard doors hanging rotted and broken from sagging hinges. Deeply puzzled, the girl looked about her, noting the ruin and desolation of the tiny homestead and yet wondering at the sense of coming home that was growing within her.

At last she stumbled to the entrance and stopped in the low doorway. Parked beside her small car was a large Land Rover. The red hair of the driver was unmistakable in the bright sunshine.

"I thought I'd find you here," said Ross at her approach. "What do you think of it?"

She turned and looked at the encircling mountains, at the azure, still waters of the little loch— and last of all at the ruined croft. "I have the strangest feeling . . . as though I'd been here before," she confessed, "and yet I've never been to Scotland before in my life."

"It happens," he said noncommittally. "Every Grannie has a store of such tales to tell." He glanced back at the house. "It's a good site for a home," he said, "with the lochan* close by and the mountains to shelter it from the weather."

He lit a cigarette and fell silent, leaning contentedly against the hood of the Land Rover.

At last she asked curiously, "Did you want me?"

He shook his head. "This is my land. I was just looking it over."

Jenna felt a faint disappointment that he hadn't come in search of her, as she had imagined at first, and looked away before he could read her expression.

"I'll be away tomorrow," he went on. "I'll leave you some work to do, and you could also catalogue the things we found in the attic." Climbing back into the Land Rover, he nodded at her as he started the engine. "See you back at the castle, Miss Clair."

*a small lake.

Standing back as he turned the vehicle, she watched as he drove off. While she had the distinct feeling that he had come with a definite purpose in view, after puzzling for a while she had to admit that she had no idea what it could be. Going back over their conversation she found no clue, try as she would and, at last, she returned to the fact that interested her most of all: with Ross Trent away, she could search for the lost 'Luck' and examine the box they had found in the attic without fear of interruption.

Eleven

Jenna awoke next morning to heavy overcast skies and damp oppressive heat. Although this was the first bad weather she had experienced since her arrival at Heron's Keep, she had become so used to blue skies and sunshine that she felt vaguely cheated and went down to breakfast in a disgruntled mood.

Alex was just finishing his meal, but he poured another cup of coffee and drank it companionably while she ate.

"Ross said he's left some papers for you to type," he told her.

"Will he be away long?"

"Only today. He's gone to Moidart to see about some cattle."

"He promised to show me the herd someday."

"They're magnificent beasties."

"Beasties? That's a strange word."

"It describes them. They're huge animals with horns like handlebars, and yet they're kindly creatures. Have you seen much of our fauna since you've been here?"

She shook her head. "Not much. I did go to Glen Clair yesterday, and saw thousands of sheep and a bird or two—but that's all. I haven't been around much."

"When's your day off? Let's make it a date and I'll take you out for the day . . . we might even see a seal or two."

"It's Wednesday—and I'd love to come!" They both laughed at her eagerness.

And then Alex asked, "Are you interested in wildlife?"

"I wasn't until I came here," she answered honestly. "I suppose I never thought about it. There's not much to see in a town, especially when one is always running to catch a bus or stealing the time to do a quick bit of shopping."

"I suppose not—Ross and I were great ones for birdwatching and studying animals when we were young." He smiled reminiscently. "Ross was a good brother to have."

"I . . . suppose so."

He looked up at her doubtful note. "Don't you get on?" he asked.

"Oh yes," she said quickly, "but I find him rather intimidating."

"He won't suffer fools, but you're hardly that, Jenna. Does he work you too hard?"

"No. It's just—that I find him rather hard to get to know. He's . . . formidable."

"He had a bad time when our mother was killed. He missed her even more than I did. And then, a while ago, a girl let him down badly. Perhaps he doesn't trust women and doesn't want to get involved again."

Reflecting that Carla seemed exempt from such feelings, Jenna was still pondering this when she left the breakfast table. Just as she turned into the corridor leading to the workrooms, she almost bumped into the American girl and drew back with a quick apology.

"Do look where you're going, Miss Clair," Carla

snapped and made to pass. Stopping suddenly and looking back over her shoulder, she said, "You won't find Mr. Trent there, you know."

"I know. He's at Moidart seeing about some cattle."

"Aren't we well informed? But then a secretary would have to know where her employer was, wouldn't she?"

"It might be useful," agreed Jenna calmly and turned to walk on down the passage.

"I expect you've lots to do. Poor little girl, I'm sure you get tired of always working."

"No, not really. I find it interesting, especially when the surroundings and people are pleasant."

This time Jenna did walk away, and closed the door of her room behind her before allowing herself to make a noise of annoyance. "The feeling's mutual, Miss Van Damm," she muttered, pulling the cover from her typewriter and looking around for the papers Ross had left her. A quick glance convinced her that they were not in her room and she went into her employer's study to see if they were there. But that room was tidy and obviously unused that morning. Puzzled, she went back to her room and looked more thoroughly. After several minutes of searching, she was sure that there were no papers left out for her to copy and she sighed in frustration, remembering his words of the previous afternoon, before she began on the catalogue of items taken from the attic.

By lunch time the skies seemed perceptibly lower and she had finished her work. Meeting Alex at the table, she asked him if he knew where his brother had left the papers.

"On your table, I think. Weren't they there? Have you looked in your room . . . shall I help?"

"I'll have another search," Jenna said hastily,

mindful of her intention to examine the box in Ross's room.

Alex proved rather eager to help but at last she got away on the pretext of a headache and hurried to her bedroom. Here, she gave the household several minutes to settle down into its afternoon peace and then cautiously opened her door. The lowering skies made the gallery unnaturally dim and the hall below was a cavern of darkness. Jenna hesitated, gathering her courage and willing herself to step out into the passage.

It took only seconds to cross to Ross's door, open it and slip inside, but to the girl those seconds seemed eternity and by the time she leaned against the closed door, her heart was hammering painfully. Almost fearfully she looked about the large room. Dark, heavy furniture stood sentinel against the walls over which textured paper rioted in splashes of cream and crimson. The same dark red was repeated in the thick Turkey carpet and full curtains hanging at the windows. A big, brass bedstead gleamed dully in the dim light. Jenna looked around, momentarily diverted by thoughts of her employer sleeping in such Victorian splendour, then recalling her self-imposed task, she glanced about more keenly.

Small and unobtrusive, the box could easily have been slipped into a drawer or cupboard, but somehow she suspected that it would be left on display and, sure enough, her questing eyes recognized the familiar shape on the dressing table, near one of the deep windows.

Silver-backed brushes stood on the pristine white linen cloth and she eyed them for a moment before, moved by some impulse she could not explain, she reached out and touched the embossed metal. Running her finger around the initials, she found herself thinking about the man who owned them and this room—so opulent and yet so masculine. Like Ross Trent himself, his room was full of contrasts.

Sighing, she picked up the box and as she did so the storm that had been threatening all day broke with frightening force. Lightning flashed across the sky, its fierce white light illuminating the room—and in the glare she saw reflected in the swinging mirror before her something she had not noticed before.

With a startled cry, she swung around to face the man sitting in the cavernous depths of the huge winged chair behind her.

"Good afternoon, Miss Clair. Have you found what you were looking for?"

Thunder crashed behind her, seeming to shake the foundations of the castle with its force and, half-blinded and deafened, Jenna crouched back against the dressing table covering her face with her hands. "I'm waiting, Miss Clair," went on the man inexorably and when she opened her eyes, she saw that he had risen and was standing in front of her, tall and commanding and as inflexible as his own castle. "I'm sure you must have a very good reason to enter my room so stealthily, and I'd like to hear it."

Speechlessly, she stared up at him. She couldn't read the expression in his eyes, but his mouth was hard and bleak. The room was very dark, almost like night and while the lightning flashed and the thunder rolled around the encircling mountains, she and Ross Trent might have been the sole inhabitants of Heron's Keep . . . and at the thought she was afraid and made a startled movement away from the immobile figure before her.

Quickly he blocked her way to the door and then, almost lazily, stretched out his arms and placed his hands on the dressing table either side of her, holding her prisoner while not touching her.

He was so close that Jenna dared not look up and she fidgeted uneasily until he bent his tall back and spoke in her ear.

"You'd best tell me, my girl . . . or you'll stay here until you do."

"It's very dark," she said inconsequently, while knowing that he was quite capable of keeping his threat and wondering miserably how to get out of the situation she had contrived for herself.

"I know . . . and I fancy you are a little afraid of thunderstorms." A long finger flicked her chin up. "Shall we go up to the roof to watch this one?" he asked wickedly.

She gasped. "You wouldn't—"

"You know I would." His hand closed about her wrist and he started towards the door.

She hung back, felt his grip tighten painfully around the fragile bones of her arm, and capitulated. "All right—I'll tell you," she said, "but let me go first."

His hand fell away, but he still stood near, his presence warning her that he was prepared to carry out his threat.

Eyeing him ruefully, she wondered how much she must tell him, remembering the old adage that half a truth is more easily believed than a whole falsehood.

"I've seen a box like that before," she began. "In fact we have one in the family just like it and there's a secret place in the lid."

"Why didn't you tell me yesterday?"

"I wanted to see for myself before I showed you." She glanced at him from under her brows and flinched at the ice in his cool grey gaze.

"Why, Miss Clair?" he asked. "What did you hope to find there?"

Jenna bit her lip, knowing she would have to tell him more. "Well . . ." she began slowly, giving herself time to think. "You remember my saying that my father was interested in Highland history? We read somewhere about your lost 'Luck.'" The man straightened abruptly at the word and she hurried on, not meeting his eyes. "And—I wondered if it might be there."

"Did you indeed?"

His voice was noncommittal and she knew that he had reservations about accepting her story. Suddenly it became imperative that he believe her and she said quickly, "Give it to me—I'll show you."

Reaching out, he picked up the box from where she had dropped it, turning it over in his fingers. "It's certainly Victorian," he murmured, "and we lost the 'Luck' about the middle of the last century." Suddenly he put it into her hands. "Do your best, Miss Clair," he told her.

Jenna opened the box, her fingers fumbling in their haste, and felt around the rim inside the lid. Her nails touched and held a small pinhead so tiny as to be unnoticeable. With difficulty, she worried at it until the head was loosened, but before she could pull it out, it twisted in her hand, breaking her nail.

Ross took the box out of her hands and removed the pin easily. "Careful, the top will fall off," she warned him and watched as he lifted the carved, inlaid top of the lid, revealing a small cavity underneath. "It is the same," she breathed. "Is there anything there?"

Peering over his arm, she sighed with disappointment at the empty space and then drew in an excited breath as he pulled out a sheet of folded paper. Going to the window, he held it so that they both could read and Jenna felt a growing sense of bewilderment as her eyes ran over the spidery writing.

* * *

My Dearest Jaimie and Alexander,

If you ever read this, I shall know that you have not forgot the games we have played together, in spite of the years that you have been away at school during which we have, perforce, grown apart.

Doubtless you will be puzzled why I have gone away, but you must seek the explanation with your father and try not to blame me too much.

I think, if you search your minds a little, you will be able to find the MacKenzie's 'Luck,' for it is ever at hand, safe under the badge of the clan and, if you find it, then I shall hear and know that you have not forgot

Your Loving Mother,
Silis MacKenzie Trent.

Jenna looked up. "What does it mean?" she asked. "Silis MacKenzie Trent?"

"She was my several times great-grandmother and ran away with her husband's overseer. This is obviously written to the children she left behind."

He spoke seemingly oblivious of the effect his words had on the girl by his side.

"She was married!" exclaimed Jenna before she could stop herself.

"Indeed she was—but what do you know about it, young lady?"

She turned away from his searching gaze and stared steadily out at the drenched mountains and steel grey sea. "Very little. Just what I've read and what my father told me. But he thought the Lady Silis married after she left here."

"I believe she did. A morganatic marriage would be a polite way of putting it. She never was divorced: people weren't in those days."

"I—see," said Jenna slowly and sighed for all her lost dreams as she tried to readjust to the fact that her family never had had a right to Heron's Keep. "How interesting."

A note of desolation in her voice made Ross study her intently and feeling his eyes on her she looked up. "I'm sorry I came into your room," she said honestly. "I shouldn't have."

"No," he agreed baldly.

Suddenly she was struck by his presence. "But—I thought you were away for the day."

A chilly smile crossed his mouth. "Did you, Miss Clair?"

Her eyes widened. "You meant me to!" she gasped.

"I had an idea you wanted to get hold of that box without me around, so I . . . provided the opportunity."

She stared at him while she struggled for words and then, somehow, she found herself on the other side of his door and almost ran along the gallery, feeling relieved to have come unscathed from the room, while the contents of Lady Silis' letter danced madly in her brain.

Twelve

Jenna pleaded a headache and missed dinner that night and avoided Ross at breakfast the next day, slipping quietly into her workroom without seeing him. Finding a pile of notes in his neat, angular writing, she set to work and was soon engrossed.

"Miss Clair." The door had opened unobserved and now Ross stood in front of her, a sheaf of papers in his hand. "I can't find the work I left for you to type yesterday. Where is it?"

"I—don't know," she stammered at a loss for words.

His eyebrows rose. "Explain, if you will."

"Alex gave me your message . . . but when I looked for the papers, I couldn't find them," she said miserably.

"Perhaps you didn't look too well—I imagine you were eager to set about your own devices."

Flushing, she hung her head. "It wasn't like that. I did look for them—but they weren't here."

"Where did you look?"

"Everywhere. Here and in your study."

"Then let us look again. How about the files, have you tried there?"

She shook her head. "I didn't know what they were."

"Try C for Clair—the factor who ran away with the Lady Silis."

"Clair!" She looked up, her eyes dark and wide.

"Yes, Miss Clair, the same name as you. Quite a coincidence, isn't it? Though as the man lived in a croft in Glen Clair, it's hardly surprising that he was called after it—to distinguish him from the other, more noble, MacKenzies." Stepping past her, he opened a drawer in the filing cabinet and flicked through the papers there. He shook his head at her inquiring glance and looked about the room. "How about that monstrous bag of yours," he asked, his eyes alighting on a gaily striped beach bag standing against the wall.

"They wouldn't be there," she protested, her voice trailing away as he opened it and took out a sheaf of crumpled papers.

"However—whoever—how did they get there?" she gasped, while her employer eyed her coldly.

"Spare me the histrionics," he begged dryly, "just type them for me—and the next time do as I ask."

"I didn't put them there."

"My dear girl, then who did? Certainly not me."

Jenna fell silent, remembering how she had met Carla in the corridor. She opened her mouth to tell him, and then caution prevailed and she decided to say nothing about what could only be a suspicion.

"No excuses, Miss Clair? Then I suggest you get back to work."

His voice was smooth and he left the room, indicating that the subject was closed. But the ease of manner that had just begun to grow between them was gone. During the next few days he hardly called Jenna into his study, instead falling into the habit of leaving notes for her on his desk each morning. She missed their former intimacy more than she liked to admit and knew that his withdrawal had more to do with her visit to his room than the loss of the papers. Apart from telling him who she was, there was nothing she could do and, distrustful of her own growing interest in her employer, she withdrew into herself, growing quiet and remote.

Alex remarked upon it on her day off, when he had collected her and driven away in the clear sparkling air.

"You've changed," he said, stopping the car in a layby on a cliff head. His eyes questioned her. "Aren't you happy? I thought you liked it here."

"I do! The country is beautiful and I—love Heron's Keep, but I feel that . . ."

"Ross can be difficult," admitted his brother, understanding her evasions. "But you're with me now. Let's forget about him for a while. I promised to try and show you some seals, and there's something down there." He pointed and, following his finger, Jenna saw an animal among the rocks where the sea swelled at the base of the cliff.

"Is it a seal?" she asked, staring at the indistinguishable grey shape.

"Either that or an otter," Alex answered, reaching for a pair of binoculars and adjusting them before he handed them to Jenna.

She peered through the glasses, surprised as rocks and cliff, grass and flowers sprang into prominence. Then she found the animal and exclaimed in delight at the cream fur and beautiful face. "He's only a baby."

"Then his mama will be somewhere around." Alex's keen eyes soon found the bigger female and, sliding his arm around Jenna's shoulders, he covered her hands with his and directed the binoculars towards the mother seal.

Suddenly conscious of his nearness, Jenna looked quickly and then offered the glasses back to her companion. "Don't you want to see?"

"I like this view," he smiled and she couldn't pretend to misunderstand what he meant.

Samantha Clare

"Why, thank you kind sir," she said demurely and felt a warm glow at his obvious admiration.

"I like a girl who accepts a compliment gracefully—Carla now, she just laps them up as if they were her due."

"She's—rather glamourous."

"I'll admit it, but it's not something I'm too keen on. Ross now, he seems to go for that kind of thing."

Jenna looked away quickly to hide the hurt she knew was in her eyes and gazed somewhat blindly out of the car window at the sea as Alex went on. "His fiancée was rather like that. She was an actress. They were going to get married. Then, just before the day, she had an offer to star in a play on Broadway." Alex shrugged. "Ross couldn't compete."

"She gave up all this?" Her gesture indicated the surrounding purple mountains and rolling sea and, behind, the way they had come. "She gave up marriage and Heron's Keep . . . and the man she loved for something so—so transient as a stage part?"

Alex was looking at her strangely. "Wouldn't you, Jenna?" he asked.

"No—if they were mine, I'd hold tight and never let them go."

Her companion reached forward and turned the ignition key. "I believe you," he commented as the car started.

The day was one of those lovely ones that occur in summer in the Western Highlands; bright and hot, with clear skies and sparkling seas. They swam in a deserted cove, ran along the white sand of its curving beach, and searched for shells and pebbles while paddling in the shallow, foaming waves. Alex took Jenna to lunch at a small hotel a little further along the shore and they ate local salmon and salad, followed by raspberries warm from the garden and fresh cream.

114

The day wore on and, in her enjoyment and wish to forget the worry and deceit behind her at the castle, Jenna didn't realize how tired she was or how hot the sun, until Alex said abruptly,

"You're pale—are you feeling the sun?"

"I have a little headache," she admitted, "but it's nothing. I expect I'm thirsty."

He stopped the car a little further on and vanished into the front door of one of a small cluster of houses. Curious, Jenna peered from her seat and saw a little collection of dusty bottles and piled tins arranged on the wide windowsill.

"We're in luck," said Alex, returning with two bottles of lemonade and a large floppy white hat, which he tossed into her lap. "We could have gone for miles and not found a shop."

"That's a shop?" smiled the girl, pulling on the hat and watching as the man forced the caps from the bottles.

"Everything one could need. From oil to flour, from washing-up powder to paint."

"Sounds enterprising," she said, accepting a drink and savouring the cool sharp taste of it as Alex swung the car back onto the road. Winding down the window, she held on to her hat and enjoyed the wind against her hot face.

"Better?" her companion asked.

"Mmm," she nodded, but in reality the dull pain behind her eyes was worse and she longed to be home and in her cool room at Heron's Keep.

When they drove into the castle courtyard the evening shadows had begun to spread purple fingers, but the air was still heavy and warm. Jenna was grateful to feel the coolness of the great hall and crossed the stone floor quickly, eager for the solitude of her room. But just as she set foot on the first stair a peremptory voice behind stopped her.

"Miss Clair!"

Obediently she turned as Ross Trent came forward out of the shadows. One look at his grim face and set mouth made her eyes open inquiringly.

"Y-es?" she asked, lifting her chin and searching for some misdemeanour of her own to account for his expression.

"Miss Clair, when I ask you to do something, I expect it to be done."

"Of course—and I've always done my best to see to it."

"Then perhaps you'll tell me why you left the work I expressly asked you to type this morning, and went out?"

She looked at him. "It was my day off."

"I am aware of that, and I explained in my note that obviously you would have another day in lieu."

"But as far as I know there was nothing to do," she went on. "I looked on your desk this morning before I went out."

"Another missing paper, Miss Clair? It seems to me that someone is being extremely careless."

"Or clever," she dared to say and watched his eyebrows raise.

"What do you mean?" he demanded impatiently.

"That someone seems to want to get rid of me."

"Oh, come now—and who do you suspect of such a dastardly plot? Me?"

"My contract is for six months, perhaps it would be handy if I left before then."

"Miss Clair, when I want you to leave, I will tell you so." He took a step nearer, eyeing her dishevelled appearance grimly and, under his cold gaze, she reached up and tugged off the floppy hat. "And, now," he went on with a certain grim amusement, "I must ask you to type my report for me."

"Tonight?" she asked, dismayed.

"Tonight," he answered inexorably. "I need to

take it with me tomorrow—you'll find it a change. Instead of history, it's about my pedigree herd."

"I'll have a bath and change first," said Jenna, preparing to climb the stairs.

His fingers closed about her hand where she clasped the newel post. Motionless she glanced down, noticing how pale and fragile her hand appeared under his and feeling how the carving of the wood cut into her palm.

"*Now*, Miss Clair," Ross said firmly, keeping his grip until he felt the compliance in her, then stepping back as she crossed the floor towards the workroom.

Staring distastefully at the sheet of figures and closely written pages, Jenna sighed for her forbidden bath, and set rather resentfully to work. The typing was difficult and required all her attention. It wasn't long before the effort started little hammers in her brain and soon the letters and figures began to dance before her tired eyes. Resolutely she continued, doggedly disciplining her fingers and ignoring the growing ache in her head until she was on the last page. With her fingers feeling like unwieldy, wooden sticks, she stared in dismay at the mistakes on the last line and wearily reached for the eraser.

"Have you finished?" inquired a voice.

"Not yet." Jenna did not look up, but lowered her eyes and hoped that Ross wouldn't notice the dangerous wobble in her own voice.

Abruptly he reached over her machine and directed the mobile lamp full onto her face.

"Don't!" she cried, shielding her eyes and dismayed to feel the scalding tears begin to slide down her cheeks. Hiding behind her hands, she sniffed dolefully and was surprised to feel a handkerchief dropped into her lap. Without a word, her employer turned her typewriter around on the table, drew up a chair and laboriously finished the last page.

"Now," he said, ripping the paper from the roller and adding it to the waiting pile. "Let's go and find some refreshment." And taking her arm above the elbow, he led her from the room.

Feeling her hesitate outside the balcony room he looked down and, sensing the reason, reassured her. "The others have gone to bed. We have the castle to ourselves. Go out onto the balcony, while I raid the kitchen."

Jenna obeyed, crossing the room full of shadows and moonlight and slipping between the gently waving curtains to feel the soft breeze that wafted in from the sea. The rough stone of the wall was cool to her hands and she leaned momentarily against it before sinking thankfully into one of the deep wicker chairs.

"Here we are," said a voice, and Ross set down a tray on a table near her. "I thought you'd prefer tea."

Jenna sipped the hot liquid appreciatively.

"There's aspirin on the tray."

Again startled by his perception, she looked up only to find his expression unfathomable in the moonlight.

"Drink your tea," he advised, his voice scarcely louder than the sea that whispered beneath the castle wall. "I've kept you up long enough."

Thirteen

After his return from his business trip Ross became much involved with his book, immersing himself and Jenna for hours in the history of Heron's Keep and the story of its many and varied inmates. Jenna found that she had little time to think of anything else and it came as quite a surprise to discover that a new entertainment was being planned.

"We're holding a conference," said Alex, invading her workroom one day. "Come and join us over coffee."

"A conference," repeated the girl, letting him take her hand and hurry her along the corridor. "What about?"

"Ross is going to give a dance for Carla . . . and she's had some mad idea—"

They had reached the balcony room and, propelled by his forceful hand, Jenna entered it more precipitously than she cared for. Ross looked up at their entrance and then settled back further in his seat.

"Let us hear what Miss Clair has to say," he said enigmatically.

"Oh, Ross honey," pouted Carla. "But I'm sure she'll agree with me."

Jenna looked quickly at the other girl, realizing

that for once the American wanted her on her side.

"I've been telling Ross about the fancy dress balls we have back home in the States. This castle is just the right setting for one, I'd say. Imagine the great hall filled with people in costume—Mary, Queen of Scots, and Bonnie Prince Charlie—What do you say?" Blue eyes regarded Jenna shrewdly. "I'd bet you've never seen one, have you?"

"Only at college and I don't suppose that's the same thing," admitted Jenna.

"The whole idea's daft!" Alex burst out. "Can you imagine Ross and me dressed as pirates or Arabs?"

"It won't be that kind of dance," Carla explained coldly. "You'll have to hire a costume. Something grand—you'd look terrific as a Highland chieftain," she finished diplomatically.

"Well, Miss Clair, what do you think?"

Jenna felt Ross's eyes upon her and stirred her coffee briskly. "I hardly know . . . it's not really for me to say."

"I asked your opinion."

"Well then—I think it's a marvellous idea." She looked up and met his gaze, her own eyes dancing with excitement. "And think of the pictures you'd get for your book," she added ingenuously.

Her employer threw up his hands in a mock gesture of surrender. "I capitulate," he laughed. "I'll leave you to arrange a date sometime in August, and you girls and Mrs. Frazer can fix all the details between you."

"Can Miss Clair type lists and things for me?" Carla asked quickly.

"I'd be pleased to," Jenna put in.

Carla gave her a dazzling smile. "And in return, I'll find you and Mrs. Frazer a vantage point to watch from. You won't mind if they sit on the gallery, will you, Ross?"

"Very much. I know Mrs. Frazer doesn't care for such things, and Miss Clair must come to the dance as a guest."

The American girl gave a brittle laugh. "Of course . . . I was joking."

"We all know your sense of humour," Alex murmured dryly and pointedly began to talk to Jenna.

Carla left soon after, followed by Alex who wanted to retune the engine of his car, having noticed a slight rattle the previous day. Jenna was left alone with Ross. Putting down her cup, she rose to leave but stood hesitating by the door. At last he looked up, his eyebrows raised inquiringly.

"Thank—thank you for inviting me to the dance," she stammered, and knew that a bright flush covered her burning cheeks.

"My pleasure," he said lightly and dismissively, and she turned and left the room, wondering why he had defended her from Carla's spite and knowing that the American girl was not one to forgive or forget a slight.

However, the next time she met Carla she found her surprisingly friendly and eager to talk.

"Come and sit with me on the terrace while I do my nails," Carla invited, leading the way out into the sunshine. "Do you know," she went on, seating herself in a lounge and arranging the polish and manicure set beside her, "when they knew I was coming here, the folks back home said I'd only need to pack raincoats and galoshes—and yet I've as good a suntan as I ever had." She looked complacently at her long brown legs, and smoothed oil over her shoulders.

Jenna watched her, leaning back with half-closed eyes while she wondered what the other girl wanted. She was sure there was some motive behind Carla's sudden friendship.

"You like it here, honey? I guess that Ross rough-rides you sometimes. How's the history going?"

"Quite well. It's very interesting work."

"Great-Aunt Katie used to write interesting letters to her sister. I remember Grandmother telling me stories—something to do with a missing good luck token, wasn't there?"

Jenna was suddenly aware that Carla's blue eyes were regarding her piercingly from behind dark glasses and she felt her heart jump alarmingly as she realized that, suddenly, they had reached the point of the other girl's desire for conversation.

"I believe the MacKenzie 'Luck' is missing," she replied guardedly.

"Just what is a 'Luck', honey? We Americans miss out on things like that."

"Usually something old—perhaps a jewel, or some object brought back from foreign parts, sometimes a flag captured at the Crusades."

"Valuable?" Carla's tone was sharp and she lifted the sunglasses, the better to see the younger girl, and not bothering to hide her own keen interest.

"Intrinsically because of its history . . . but even more so to the clan to whom it belongs."

"And nobody knows where the MacKenzie one is?"

"I don't think so."

"Ross told me that he'd found a letter about it the other day. I guess he's very keen to find it."

"I imagine so," answered Jenna thoughtfully and was still deep in thought when she left Carla sunning herself on the terrace.

An uneasy truce still existed between them when, a few days later, Ross offered them both a lift into town to get some things they needed for the dance.

"Bring a bag, honey, there'll be a lot to carry. We need invitations and cards, and decorations for the table," advised Carla, who obviously had no intentions of carrying any of the items she named.

Their new-found amiability lasted until after Ross had dropped them and driven off, and then a chance remark from Jenna destroyed whatever hope there had been of a friendship between them.

"Have you seen the dresses we found up in the attics?" she asked. "Mr. Trent wants me to wear one while it's being photographed for his book."

Carla stopped abruptly and spun around. "Oh, does he now? And how come you're always around when he wants anything done? Are you making up to him?"

Jenna blinked, surprised by the other's attack. "Of course not! It's just that I happen to be the right size."

"I'll have you remember that you just work at Heron's Keep—and don't get ideas above your station."

Jenna's chin set rebelliously and, reading mutiny in her face, Carla glared down at her, blue eyes alight in her tanned face. "See here, sweetie, I can make things pretty uncomfortable for you if I like. I have a good deal of influence, you know."

The younger girl stared back, swallowing her resentment as she realized the truth in her opponent's words. Undoubtedly, Ross would listen to his cousin and suddenly Jenna knew that she wanted to stay at the castle more than she had ever wanted anything before. Dropping her gaze, she said in a conciliatory voice, "I don't know really what you mean, but . . ."

"Just think of your position at the castle as a job, honey . . . a passing job, and don't get any ideas about your employer." A moment longer the icy blue eyes stared at Jenna and then, evidently assuming that she was sufficiently subdued, Carla went on,

"Now we understand each other, let's go shopping."

Without waiting to see if the other was following, she led the way into various shops, choosing items and handing them to Jenna to carry with cool arrogance.

Quite suddenly the English girl had had enough. "There's someone I know," she cried, with what she hoped was well-simulated excitement. "I must talk to her!" And, not waiting to see Carla's response, she dashed hastily away, threading her way through convenient groups of tourists until Carla was lost to sight. Rather pleased with her subterfuge, Jenna hurried away from the thronged thoroughfare and, seeing a small café with dark furniture and bright red and white checked curtains, she dodged inside choosing a table with a good view of the street outside. She sat down and ordered tea.

Knowing that Ross Trent was not picking them up until half-past four, she lingered over the meal, enjoying the scones and jam and squeezing the last drop of tea from the pot. Then, looking at her watch, she paid her bill and went in search of the clock tower where they were all to meet. She arrived just in time to see her employer's large car sweep past her, skirt the tower and glide away out of sight. It happened so quickly that she had only half started to make a gesture to attract his attention before the car was gone, leaving her stunned and puzzled.

She was almost sure that Carla had seen her: those blue eyes had flickered in her direction before the American tossed her blonde hair and said something to the man beside her. Nevertheless, Jenna waited on the pavement for a while, half-expecting them to come back. At last she guessed her hope was unfounded and began to wonder what to do.

A quick search in her purse made her wish that

she hadn't spent so much on the material for her fancy dress. She knew Alex was out for the day, trying out his car, so he couldn't come to her rescue. A taxi would have been the answer, but she had no cash. A bus stopped opposite and drew noisily away as Jenna eyed it with sudden interest. It was the work of minutes to find out the nearest route to the castle. By good fortune a bus stop was near and a bus due, and soon she was seated in a crowded vehicle that shuddered and roared along the road Ross's car had covered so effortlessly earlier.

The bus route meandered between villages and alongside mountains and burns until Jenna lost all sense of direction and time, only knowing that the journey had taken what seemed like hours. Presently the bus jerked to a halt and the driver shouted that this was her stop. Hastily she scrambled to her feet, clutching her shopping bag, and clambered over feet and parcels to the entrance. The driver pointed out the direction for her to take and then drove off, leaving her alone with a cloud of diesel fumes and several sheep.

As she began to walk along the road, heavy drops of rain spotted the tarmac at her feet and soon began to fall quickly. Jenna buttoned her thin jacket and wished for a raincoat, while her bag became heavier and her surroundings more desolate.

She had reached a bend in the road and Heron's Keep lay below her, looking like a boy's toy fort at that distance, when she heard the welcome sound of an engine behind her and turned quickly, her hand raised hopefully.

The Land Rover stopped beside her and its driver regarded her, showing no surprise at her appearance on the remote road.

"It'll be Miss Clair, I'm thinking. You'd like a lift no doubt."

"Yes, please," said Jenna simply, and climbed thankfully into the empty seat beside the factor, shivering in her wet suit.

"There's a jacket behind you, if you'd care to put it on," said Euan MacKenzie, starting the car again.

"I've been into town," explained the girl, huddling gratefully into the warmth of the coat, "and Mr. Trent was to pick me up, but something must have gone wrong and he drove off without me. I got as far as here on a bus."

The factor frowned. "That doesn't sound like Mr. Trent," he commented briefly. "It's lucky that I came along. It's quite a way to the castle and the rain is heavy now." He glanced at her bulging bag. "Are the things you bought spoiled?"

"I don't think so. I pushed them well down—I'm the only thing that got wet!" She brushed the damp hair back from her face and laughed a little.

"You'll be liking it here?"

"I love it!"

"And the history of the old house—you find it interesting?"

"Very." Jenna realized that the man had adjusted the driving mirror slightly and was watching her in it. For a moment their reflected eyes met and then he looked away, concentrating on the road ahead.

"No doubt you've found out about the old stories and legends. I believe there are enough to fill a book."

"Y-es," Jenna answered warily, feeling that she had held this conversation before. "Mr. Trent has told me quite a few."

"Buried treasure and so on. We all used to be pirates at one time."

"No, not treasure . . . but he did tell me about the lost 'Luck' of the MacKenzies," she said boldly, watching for his reaction and noting how his hands tightened almost imperceptibly on the steering wheel.

"Ah . . . and you've found no clue to its whereabouts?"

He guided the Land Rover under the archway and brought it to a halt beside the castle steps, turning to look at his passenger with the engine still running.

Jenna picked up her bag and avoided answering him. "Thank you, Mr. MacKenzie," she said, "you've been very kind."

He lifted a hand in acknowledgement and drove off as she started up the steps. Something made her glance back before pushing open the door and again she met his eyes, before she hastily opened the door and went into the castle.

Fourteen

"Well, what happened to you?" asked Alex as she crossed the hall. "Have you just washed your hair, or did you get caught in the rain?"

Jenna glowered at him and was even more annoyed to see Carla standing beside him, a gleam of triumph in her eyes.

"Didn't your friend give you a lift after all?" she inquired sympathetically.

"I was mistaken," Jenna answered shortly. "It wasn't a friend at all. I think you might have waited for me, not just driven off like that, leaving me stranded."

"But darling—after you didn't come back, what could I think, but that you'd found your friend and were making your own way home?"

"So I did . . . on a bus and then the overseer gave me a lift."

"Then all's well," cooed Carla sweetly, while Alex looked from one to the other, puzzled by the undercurrents in their conversation.

"Here's the things you wanted," went on Jenna, dumping the bag at the other girl's neatly shod feet. "I hope the wet hasn't ruined them. I'm afraid I won't have time to do any typing for you today—I'll have to set my hair and dry it." She marched up the stairs, conscious of the concerted gazes of the other two on her back, and shut herself in her room to allow her temper to cool.

She sat silent at dinner that evening—answering when spoken to, but not joining in the conversation—although Carla seemed in a particularly vivacious mood, making both Alex and Ross laugh with her account of a holiday spent on a Dude Ranch in Arizona.

After the meal, Jenna made her excuses and escaped to her room. Impulsively, she changed into trousers and thick shoes, dragged on a raincoat and, snatching up a head scarf, slipped out of the castle.

The rain had slowed to little more than a heavy mist as she crossed the courtyard, though water lay deep in the crannies between the cobblestones. Under the archway she hesitated for a second and then turned away from the road that led to the town, heading towards the path to Glen Clair, though she had no intention of walking as far as the croft.

At first she walked with her head down, watching her feet as they rhythmically appeared at the edge of her raincoat skirt but after a while her mood lightened and, raising her eyes, she began to take an interest in her surroundings, noticing how fresh the colours were after the reviving rain. And how drops of water showered away from the grass with each footfall.

The road edged slowly upwards and soon she could look back and downwards to the rock that held Heron's Keep. The sweet smell of heather rose from the hillside, reminding her of the honey her father used to buy as a special treat. She bent to pick a purple-pink spray and tucked it into a buttonhole before leaving the road to take the rough track between the mountains that headed to the croft in the glen.

The rain had turned the ground into a quagmire—thick, sticky mud and deep puddles fighting for a place among the big stones that littered the path. Soon her shoes were coated and heavy, making each step difficult and uncomfortable. She was almost on the point of turning back, when the sound of an engine made her look around. Balancing precariously on a flattish boulder, she waited for the vehicle to draw level, and watched as Ross Trent leaned across the empty seat to open a door.

"Get in!" he said briefly.

Quite suddenly, she wanted to go on as much as she had wanted to turn back before. "No, thank you," she answered perversely, "I'm going for a walk."

"My dear girl, it's raining. Dusk is coming and you'll be both wet and lost."

She considered. "Then I'll walk back. I can't get lost, and if I get wet then that's my own affair."

Abruptly he changed his tactics. "Get in, there's a good girl. I want to talk to you."

Jenna eyed him and found herself subjected to the full effect of his charm. Grey eyes smiled at her as he held out his hand invitingly. Somewhat shaken, she allowed herself to be drawn into the car, leaning back and pulling off her wet scarf as the car was turned expertly and headed back towards the main road.

At the junction she was surprised when Ross swung around, taking the road away from Heron's Keep.

"Where are we going?" she asked involuntarily.

"Afraid of being kidnapped, Miss Clair?" asked the man, glancing at her quickly before turning his attention back to the winding road that showed like a white ribbon in the growing dusk.

"Should I be?" she countered, matching his mood.

Ross shook his head. "Not today. Like you, I feel the need to get away from the castle for a while."

"Were you looking for me?" asked Jenna, curious as to how he had found her so easily.

"Alex saw you go," her companion explained briefly, stopping the car on a flat patch of white gravel surrounding a long, low building that stood beside a smooth stretch of water.

"This is a hotel," he said, "noted for its cuisine. I find the atmosphere congenial." Swinging his long legs to the ground, he came around to Jenna's side and opened the door for her, taking her arm as he led her to the front door that stood invitingly open.

Jenna stood in the entrance and looked around the dark, paneled room. Furnished with settles and long tables, with a cheerful fire at one end, it appeared more like a private room than a hotel.

"Sit down, and I'll arrange about refreshments."

She watched as Ross, who evidently knew his way around, vanished through a door in the far wall. Then realizing how cold and damp she was, she went towards the fire and sat in one of the settles that flanked either side.

"The landlord will bring them in a minute," said Ross, returning. "Give me your coat and I'll put it to dry."

By the time he had arranged the garment to catch the warmth, a rotund man with a tray had arrived and smiled at them both.

"It's good to see you, Mr. Trent," he beamed.

"And you, Ferguson—how's trade?"

"Not so bad. Good in the season—and we even manage a few visitors during the rest of the year." Putting down the tray, he smiled and nodded his way from the room, leaving Jenna and Ross alone.

The girl stretched her legs to the fire, eyeing her steaming trousers, uneasily aware of the man beside her.

"There's sandwiches and coffee and a wee drop of Drambuie to keep the cold away," he said suddenly, and for a while they ate and drank in silence. He waited until she leaned back clasping the small thin glass of liqueur—when he spoke, turning towards her, one arm along the high back of the settle behind her.

"Alex tells me that there was some mix-up over my collecting you and Carla this afternoon."

"Yes . . . I thought I'd seen someone I knew . . ."

"Someone important?"

"Not really—just someone from college." She looked up fleetingly, disliking telling him a lie, and found his eyes disquietingly intent.

"I'm sorry you were left stranded."

"That's all right—it was really my fault," she assured him, relieved to be able to speak the truth. "I found a bus, and then Mr. MacKenzie gave me a lift."

"You're a very enterprising young woman," her companion smiled.

Suddenly aware of his nearness, Jenna sat up straight and took an unwary gulp of her drink. The sweet, fiery liquid caught at her throat and she swallowed convulsively, blinking away tears and trying to hide her discomposure. Although other people had come into the room, the high back of the settle shut them off, making Ross's presence at once companionable and . . . disturbing.

She turned to say something—anything—to break the growing tension she sensed between them and found him unexpectedly close, his grey eyes clear and bright, reminding her of the rain-swept pool she had passed earlier that evening. Spinning her empty glass between her fingers, she looked quickly away, feeling a nerve jump in her throat.

"Come, Miss Clair—relax!" Ross urged. "I half expect you to leap to your feet and run from the room." He drew the glass out of her unresisting fingers and then carried her hands to her lap, holding them there in a firm grip. "Nothing to say?" he asked. "And yet you're not usually silent. Surely you're not nervous of me?"

Aware of his charm, Jenna knew that he had set himself to win her approval and suddenly raised her head to meet his gaze questioningly.

"Not nervous—puzzled," she said as steadily as the uneven beating of her heart would allow. "Why have you brought me here?"

"Does a man need a reason to take out a pretty girl?" he asked lazily, leaning back in his corner, half turned to face her.

"I should be flattered," she replied impishly, "until now I've been treated as an employee—"

"Relationships change," he told her. "We meet people and get to know them—then either we pass on . . . or a friendship grows and develops." His light eyes smiled into hers, aware of the speculation in their depths. "Alex has used your first name for some time. May I call you Jenna?"

"Please . . . please do."

"And Ross isn't difficult to say."

"Ross," she repeated obediently, remembering the times it had been on her mind while she called him by the formal title.

He looked up at a sudden commotion behind them and then rose reluctantly.

"Closing time," he remarked. "We'd best go with a good grace, though the law isn't enforced too vigorously about here."

He helped her on with the now dry and warm coat, lifting the heavy strands of her hair away from the collar. For a moment his hands seemed to linger beside her neck. Calling goodnight to the landlord, he guided her out into the night, still quite light now that the rain clouds had dispersed. The air was sweet and soft after the rain and they both lifted their heads into it appreciatively.

"The night's young yet." He turned impulsively to her, looking down from his height. "Shall we go for a walk?"

"I'd love to," she answered readily. "If you remember, that's what I was doing when you abducted me."

"Then the least I can do is to show you part of our coastline. This is the island part of our loch. This water passed Heron's Keep a few hours ago."

Tucking her hand into the crook of his elbow, he covered her fingers with his other hand and led her across the gravel towards the water's edge. The loose shingle and sand gave pleasantly beneath their feet, crunching delightfully with each step. Jenna tried to match her strides to his, but had to give up, laughing and panting as he obligingly shortened his step to match hers.

The moon turned the white sand to silver, edging the lazy sea with filigree, while the trees that bounded the shore looked like delicate black lace.

Jenna sighed. "Oh . . . it's beautiful! What a lovely country."

Ross stood still and turned her to face him, his hands hard on her arms just below her shoulders. "You like it here?" he asked, his breath fanning her cheek.

She looked up, her face pale in the moonlight, while her eyes were deep pools of shadow. The breeze lifted a strand of hair across her cheek and he raised one hand to smooth it away.

"I love it here," she breathed, very conscious of his nearness and lifting her face to his touch.

His fingers were cool and hard and slightly abrasive, and she was reminded that he farmed his land, working beside his overseer and men at times.

"You look like Pygmalion," he murmured softly. "A woman of stone—shall I bring you to life?"

His mouth hovered nearer and Jenna caught her breath as she closed her eyes. The moment grew long and her lids fluttered open. Instead of kissing her, Ross Trent was regarding her intently, his head back the better to examine her.

"Why did you come to Heron's Keep?" he asked quietly.

Her mouth opened and she licked suddenly dry lips, while her heart began such a crescendo in her chest that she felt he would hear it.

"To—for the job," she stammered, stepping back and trying to break his grip.

"I'd be grateful for the truth."

Something in his voice made her still and she glanced up fleetingly, biting her lip, while he looked down at her, his face hidden by shadows.

"I . . . don't know what you mean," she breathed, feeling his fingers tighten and bite into her arms.

"Don't play with me." His voice was harsh and, in his impatience, he shook her slightly. "You're more than naturally interested in the history of my home. Scotland is a long way for a girl like you to come to find a job—there must be hundreds in the south that suited you as well. There's something—mysterious about you, Miss Clair."

She took a breath and fought down the panic rising in her and then her ready temper came to her rescue and she determined to outface him. "I'm sorry you feel like that," she said with a semblance of calm. "Perhaps I'd better leave."

She was unaware of the note of desolation that had crept into her voice at the prospect. Ross looked down at the girl drooping in his hands, and his expression softened slightly at the sight of a single tear making a snail track down the smooth surface of her cheek.

"You've a contract," he reminded her. "You'll leave when I tell you to—or when the period named is over. Until then you'll work for me." His teeth gleamed suddenly in the bright light from the moon. "And I'll do my damnedest to find out what puzzles me about you, Miss Jenna Clair."

Fifteen

Ross's words were still ringing in Jenna's ears when she woke the next morning and she lay still, painfully reviewing the events of the previous night, remembering the blaze of anger she had felt when she realized that he had no intention of kissing her and had, in fact, only taken her out for the opportunity of questioning her.

Scrambling out of bed, she showered quickly, put on her most severe dress in spite of the clear skies and bright sun beyond her windows, and tied back her hair at the nape of her neck with a black scarf. Then, feeling the very epitome of an efficient secretary, she went downstairs.

Breakfast was a strained meal and she was glad to escape to her workroom and find oblivion in the notes on her desk and the swift tap of typewriter keys. Suppressed bad temper gave such impetus to her fingers that she had finished her work well before the time coffee could be found in the balcony room, and rather than seek Ross and ask if he had any more work for her as she knew she should do, she wandered from room to room and, at last, found herself beside the white piano. Suddenly realizing that she had not played for days, she longed to touch the ivory keys and almost before she knew what she was doing, she was seated and her fingers were rippling over the keyboard.

137

Usually she liked romantic music: Chopin and Debussy were her favourite composers, but now she felt the need for something stronger, more emotional and—louder! Her fingers slid into Beethoven and the thunderous chords rang out, making the room reverberate and giving her great satisfaction. As the last notes died away, she lifted her hands from the keys, massaging her aching fingers and resolving to practice more.

"Now that's out of your system, come out onto the terrace. It's a lovely morning and too good to miss."

Jenna looked up quickly and then smiled at Alex, perched on the edge of a desk near the windows. "I didn't hear you come in."

"I know you didn't. You were very intense and enrapt. I only hope I'm not the cause when you feel the need of a piece by Wagner!"

She laughed and got up, feeling her mood lighten. "Don't you like Beethoven?" she asked.

"Not at ten-thirty in the morning—the timing's wrong. It's like having a tipple before the sun's over the yardarm, or opening one's presents before Christmas."

She considered. "Perhaps you're right, though just then *he* seemed right."

Alex held back the curtain. "Let's go outside."

Gulls wheeled and dipped overhead, making Jenna think of her first meeting with the enigmatic Ross and her first sight of Heron's Keep. Feeling an unfamiliar snatch of pain in her heart, she turned to Alex to quiet her own thoughts, and asked quickly,

"Your leg—it's better? I mean . . . you hardly limp now, only when you're tired and even then not much."

He looked out to sea, his profile sharp against the azure sky, the wind ruffling his fair hair. "I guess it's almost time for me to leave my refuge," he admitted.

"Do you like it here so much?" she asked, and he spun around to lean his back against the stone wall, thrusting both hands into his pockets as he grinned at her.

"I'd reached an impasse," he confessed. "I'd been to University not really knowing what I wanted to do—wasted my time and failed the exams. The only thing I was any good at was skiing. I'd even hoped I might go to the next Olympics." He shrugged and smiled slightly, "Well, my accident took care of that."

"You mean you won't be able to ski again?" the girl asked, the sympathy she felt very evident in her voice.

"Not in first class competitions." His tone was matter-of-fact and she slowly realized that it was of very little importance to him. His voice was enthusiastic when he went on. "I've been here for the longest time since I went away to school . . . and do you know, Jenna, I've suddenly found out what I want to do with my life. I've always been interested in biology and the local flora and fauna—I'm going to take a degree in forestry and then come back here and help Ross run the estate. He wants to bring out the forestry side of it and it would be just the thing for me."

Jenna looked up, her eyes shining. "Oh, Alex, how wonderful!" she exclaimed. "I'm so glad for you."

"Well, it'll be a lot of hard work, but worth it, I'm sure."

"How lovely to stay here for always."

"You've taken to this part of the country, haven't you?"

"It's as if I've lived here always," she told him simply. "If I—*when* I leave, part of me will stay here."

"Did you enjoy your walk last night? Ross was worried about you when he found that you were out."

Now it was Jenna's turn to gaze at the sea with

unseeing eyes, as she heard Alex tell her that his brother had unsettled the castle looking for her until he'd been told that she had been seen heading towards the Glen Clair road. So, she thought, he had not just followed her to ask questions and find out the answers to the mystery he half suspected.

"I can tell you, he was annoyed with Carla for leaving you behind in town," Alex went on, oblivious to her confused thoughts. "At one time I thought that they'd make a go of it, but now he seems to have gone off her somewhat. Now, why do you think that is?"

Realizing that he was waiting for an answer, Jenna looked up and met his teasing eyes. "I'm sure I don't know," she said quietly, while her mind reeled with speculation. If Ross's own brother suspected she was the cause, then surely she might be allowed a little surmise herself?

She was still in this aberrant state of mind when she went back to her workroom and had only been there a few mintues when Carla appeared in the doorway.

"Mind if I come in?"

Jenna eyed the beige trouser suit and the ingratiating face above it. "Not at all," she said politely, wondering at the reason behind this unexpected visit, "but I'm very busy." To prove her words, she pulled out a filing drawer and began to go through the contents in an efficient manner.

Carla moved restlessly about the room, touching the keys of the typewriter with one long, varnished nail, flicking over the pages Jenna had typed, and glancing at the other girl warily now and again when she thought she was unobserved.

Jenna pushed the drawer shut and opened another. "Carla," she said, flipping through the reference cards, "do you want something?"

"How perceptive, honey," said the other at once,

obviously pleased with the opening provided. "It's my hair—did you ever see such a mess?" She dragged her fingers through her blonde tresses dramatically, while waiting for Jenna's denial. When none came, she went on quickly, hiding the tiny flash of resentment she felt. "I must get it done, but everyone is out. Ross has vanished somewhere and Alex is out playing with his car again—and I'm stuck . . . unless . . ."

"You want me to drive you into town?"

"I wouldn't want to take you away from your work, darling. No, if you'd just lend me your car for a while. Oh, it's all right. I've a driving license and you're insured, aren't you?"

"Well . . . I don't know."

"Be a poppet—"

Jenna looked at the American girl, realizing that she never doubted the outcome of her demand. All her life her desires had been met and she had no doubts that Jenna would do as she wished. Quite suddenly Jenna was tired of the subject; Carla was a disturbing influence in the room and she wanted to be alone and think about . . . Ross.

"Here are the keys," she said suddenly, taking them out of her handbag and dropping them into the outstretched palm. "Be careful, won't you?"

Carla blew her a kiss from the door. "You're a doll," she told her before striding away.

A frown appeared between Jenna's eyes. Surely there was something she should have told the other girl? She pondered for a few seconds then, unable to recall the elusive memory, mentally shrugged and turned back to her filing cabinet.

Forgetting about Carla and battling with her own disturbing thoughts, Jenna worked through the afternoon and it wasn't until after dinner that evening that she remembered what she had meant to tell Carla.

"Carla's late," murmured Alex, briskly stirring his coffee. "I wonder where she can be?"

"She's gone to have her hair done," Jenna supplied and the memory struck her like a blow. "Oh good grief!" she gasped, and at that moment the phone in the hall rang.

One look at Ross's face when he returned told her that she was right in her surmise.

"That was Carla," he said curtly. "I'm going to pick her up." His eyes travelled grimly over the girl looking apprehensively up at him, and even Jenna realized how guilty she must look. "Don't run away, Miss Clair. None of your walks or sick headaches if you please. I want a word with you when I return."

"What's biting him?" asked his brother when they were alone. "He's more bedeviled than a blue-tailed fly lately." He looked more closely at Jenna. "What have you been up to? You look the picture of guilt."

Avoiding his eyes, she said, "Nothing." And then more truthfully, "I lent Carla my car—and forgot to tell her the tank was almost empty."

Alex's hoot of laughter filled the room, making even the wires of the piano reverberate.

"I don't see why it makes you laugh," she said crossly.

"Oh, Lord, I'd have liked to see her face! I bet she was mad. I don't blame you at all, my pet. I'd have done the same thing if I'd had the opportunity."

She looked at him aghast and, when she could speak, said quickly, "I didn't do it deliberately—I forgot."

"I'm sure you did," he agreed hastily, breaking into laughter again. "Never mind, don't look so downcast—I'll take your part."

Somehow his words didn't comfort the girl as they should have. She strongly suspected that he would be no match for his elder brother, and was soon to find her fears well-founded.

The next half hour passed all too quickly for Jenna. She had only prowled around the room a few times when the sound of a returning car made her pause in her stride and listen as doors slammed and feet ran across the great hall and upstairs.

Ross appeared in the doorway and strode purposefully towards her. "Come along, Miss Clair," he said, taking her wrist in a steely grip. "Time for our little talk."

"I say, Ross—" began Alex, true to his word, but his brother marched imperiously from the room with Jenna willy-nilly in his wake and did not stop until they were in his study.

Still holding her, he reached behind his back to lock the door, dropping the key into his pocket. "Just so that we won't be disturbed," he told her, his eyes glittering. Seeing the glint of grey ice in his gaze, Jenna felt her heartbeat quicken at his anger.

"Now perhaps you'll tell me what you mean by deliberately sending Miss Van Damm out in a car without enough petrol to get back?"

"Let me go!" She tugged at his fingers and, finding this ineffectual, made the statement that would surely ensure her release: "You're hurting me."

For answer his grip tightened, warning her that he really could hurt her if he wished, and she stifled a sudden gasp of fright. "When you've answered my question," he said inexorably, and waited for her reply.

She shuffled her feet and hung her head, unwilling to give in. "You—we can hardly stay here all night."

Leaning back against the door, he gave an impression of immovability. "Why not?" he asked, and Jenna read his implacable mood and shrugged off her pride.

"I didn't," she said. "I honestly forgot—until just now after dinner when Alex asked where she was."

"Do you expect me to believe that?"

"Why not? It's the truth."

"Carla told me how vindictive you've been about her mistake in thinking you had arranged a lift back from town."

"Vindictive! Why she's the one—treating me like a maid, wanting me to do errands for her and making snide remarks about how wealthy she is and how poor and insignificant I am."

He looked down at her, his face cold. Dropping her wrist, he said, "She told me you had a chip on your shoulder and were jealous of her."

Rubbing her wrist, she closed her mouth, biting back the words as she realized that whatever she said now would only make matters worse.

"She's clever," she muttered, swinging away and going to stare blankly out of the window, "but you might at least give me a hearing."

"I don't think there's much to be said."

Suddenly she spun around, hair flying and eyes blazing as her temper rose. "Oh, don't you. Well, we'll see about that! Just who do you think you are, Mr. Ross MacKenzie-Trent? Some lord in your castle, with the poor sitting around at the gate waiting for any crumb of kindness you might drop when it's not too much trouble? I'll tell you, Mr. Trent, that I'm not a member of your clan or sept or whatever—I'm a freeborn woman and I won't be treated like a—a serf. You're the most arrogant and infuriating man I've ever met!"

He unlocked the door and stood back. "You may go, Miss Clair," he said softly, and his very quietness should have warned Jenna.

"May I? Just because you don't like a few home truths—"

"On the contrary, the truth is what I'd be very keen to hear."

His words made her stop and take a breath, and look at him. His eyes were very keen and bright and she felt her rage dwindling under the scrutiny. "I'd best leave in the morning," she said dully, turning away.

"Oh, no," he answered quietly, his voice so full of menace that she felt the hair on the back of her neck lift as a chill ran down her spine. "You'll not leave here until I say so."

Startled eyes flew to his, her expression half panic-stricken, wholly poised for flight.

He smiled without amusement. "I shan't lock you in a dungeon . . . but be very sure I'd sue you for breach of contract . . . and I'd make sure you had great difficulty in getting another job."

With shaking hands Jenna fumbled at the door handle, but he hadn't finished with her yet.

"Another thing," his voice was cold and curt and she bowed her shoulders and leaned her forehead against the door, held a prisoner by his hard tones. "Use what sense you have and learn to curb that temper of yours . . . and, if you'll take my advice, you'll remember that Carla is my cousin, and happens to be a guest at Heron's Keep."

The meaning of his words was very clear. Jenna tugged at the door and ran from the room, his words echoing in her brain.

Scalding tears blinded her as she ran up the stairs; nothing Ross said could have made it plainer how he regarded her. To him she was an employee— nothing more, and she knew suddenly and with great clarity that he was more important to her than all her ambitions to find the 'Luck' and stay at the castle. Suddenly she admitted to herself that she was in love with the owner of Heron's Keep . . . and the knowledge brought no comfort at all.

Sixteen

By the next time Jenna saw her employer, her pride had come to the rescue and she was able to meet him with a tolerable semblance of composure and assumed indifference.

Arriving in the balcony room and finding herself early for breakfast, she wandered out onto the terrace only to find herself confronted by his formidable back as he leaned over the wall. Hesitating in the doorway, she would have drawn back, but he spoke without moving.

"Come here," he said quietly.

Curious, she approached and was drawn forward by his arm and urged to look downward at the deep sea at the base of the rock on which the castle stood.

"What is it?" she whispered, watching the slim, lithe animal as it swam and pirouetted in the water, small paws held close to its face.

"An otter," he answered briefly, his eyes watching its antics as it swam and played with obvious enjoyment. It gambolled beneath them a few minutes more, then flipping over, it headed quickly away, moving towards the inland shore of the loch. "We don't often see them down as far as this," Ross said, turning to lean against the wall.

"I've never seen one before."

"They used to be more plentiful, but with hunts and dogs, there aren't as many as there were. I don't allow hunting on my land. If there's a rogue fox or deer to be culled we go after it with guns and kill it cleanly, not make a sport of it."

"I can imagine that you would be very efficient and not . . . sentimental."

For the first time that morning, he really looked at her. "There's no room for sentiment in a farmer's life, Miss Clair." When she would have moved away, he reached out and caught her arm. "And that's how our relationship will be from now on. Efficient, businesslike and with no sentiment."

Shrugging herself free from his hold, she faced him steadily. "When was it ever anything else?" she asked coldly, lifting her chin, her eyes stormy with suppressed emotion.

Hearing Alex come into the room behind them, she broke away from Ross thankfully and hurried towards the door. He caught up with her at the entrance to the balcony room and held the curtain aside for her.

"We've a busy day ahead," he reminded her as she made to pass him. When he went on she kept her face lowered so that he was forced to talk to the top of her glossy head. "I want you to take notes for me this morning when I visit the farm, and this afternoon the photographer is coming to take shots to illustrate my book."

Nodding, she murmured her compliance and crossed in front of him, taking her place at the table and noticing with surprise that Carla had joined them for breakfast. The American girl glanced at her curiously a few times, her blue eyes alight with speculation, but obviously she could derive no satisfaction from either her or Ross's manner. On becoming aware that Ross and Jenna would be occupied for most of the day, she turned her attention to Alex, flattering and cajoling him into taking her out to lunch.

"My car's not fit for a run yet," he protested.

"Take mine—I'll be using the Land Rover today," said his brother, and Jenna saw a quick glance pass between them before Alex agreed, making little attempt to conceal his reluctance.

However, Carla appeared not to notice, sending Jenna a quick glance of triumph before loudly beginning to make plans and discuss suitable places of refreshment.

"Why not go to the hotel Mr. Trent took me to?" Jenna was unable to resist saying. "It seemed a very nice place—cosy and secluded. I'm sure you'd like it."

Alex looked up, his eyes alight with laughter. "Where was that, Ross?" he asked.

"Ferguson's place, the other end of the loch," the elder man answered briefly, but Jenna thought his mouth half curved in a smile as he bent again over his plate.

No one seemed keen to linger over the meal and soon Carla left the room. Ross stood up, dropping his napkin on the table and looking inquiringly at the remaining girl. Jenna hastily swallowed the last of her coffee and followed him, fortified by a huge wink from Alex as he watched them go.

"Trousers and a warm jacket," advised her employer as they crossed the hall. "I'll see you in the courtyard in ten minutes' time."

She watched him stride off towards his study and then hurried upstairs to change and find a coat. She took less than the allotted time, but even so Ross was seated in the driving seat of the big vehicle, waiting as she ran down the steps.

With one hand on the steering wheel, he reached the other to help her. Jenna was unprepared for the strong pull and arrived precipitously in the seat beside him as he turned the ignition key and started the engine.

"We'll pick up MacKenzie first," he explained as they passed under the archway and stopped a few yards on, beside the huddle of houses alongside the road.

The overseer must have been waiting for them because he came out almost at once and, after greeting them, climbed into the back of the vehicle. Jenna clutched the edge of her seat as they started off again, feeling her teeth jar as they left the tarmac road and lurched along an unmade-up track. The height of the Land Rover compensated for the discomfort of the ride, however, and she looked about with interest as they climbed between the mountains, black-faced sheep darting away at their approach.

Soon the encircling hills opened out into a flat plain with a cluster of buildings tucked under one side. The Land Rover was drawn off the track and parked beside a whitewashed wall, but when both men climbed out Jenna realized why Ross and his overseer were wearing heavy rubber boots; the track and surrounding farmyard were a sea of thick, sticky mud.

She hesitated, wondering if there could be some possible way around her difficulty, but after scanning her surroundings she was forced to admit defeat and call for help.

Ross turned at once and, leaving the group of men he'd been talking to, came back.

"You said trousers and a jacket—but nothing about footwear."

He glanced down at her neat brogues. "I'll carry you," he said curtly, and before she could protest had reached into the car and scooped her into his arms.

Jenna had a confused impression of a brown cheek near hers, a faint smell of after-shave and an almost delicious feeling of helplessness, before she was tossed up onto a farm truck and her employer was calling for a bale of hay for her to sit on.

"I hope you didn't drop your notebook," he threw over his shoulder. A gleam in his eye telling her that he was well aware of her agitation when she had found herself in his arms.

Movement behind her and a snort of warm breath made her turn quickly to find that the truck had been drawn close against a barred gate through which several pairs of curious eyes above moist, soft noses were regarding her. With a murmur of delight, she dropped to her knees, holding out a hand only to have the half-grown Highland heifers shuffle away. Eventually, after much coaxing, one came forward, accepted a twist of hay from her hand and allowed her to rub its shaggy head while it ate.

"You're not afraid of cattle?"

She looked up to see the overseer standing near, watching her. She shook her head. "Not really—though I don't think I'd be too keen if I found myself in a field with a bull."

"Ah, these are soft creatures—real gentle beasties." He climbed up onto the truck and reached his hand to scratch a head, and she noticed that his attention was accepted eagerly, not with suspicion as hers had been.

"You're good with animals, I can see."

"I've worked with them all my life," he answered simply.

"And how long have you worked for Mr. Trent?"

"Ever since I left college. I'm a MacKenzie, Miss Clair, this is my home."

It was obviously unthinkable that he should ever live elsewhere and Jenna looked at his bent head, wondering at such love of birthplace and loyalty to clan. Then, remembering the effect Heron's Keep had on herself, she began to feel the stirrings of understanding grow within her. Her reflections were disturbed by a shout from her employer telling her to have her pencil poised and, from then on, the morning was a rush of taking notes and filling pages with remarks and lists of numbers, none of which she understood in the least.

At last the hubbub died down; voices were quiet and the endless procession of animals stopped, and Jenna dared to put down her pencil and rub her chilled fingers.

"We could do with a drink," said Ross. "Let's see if there's one to be had at the house." He tossed a well worn pair of Wellington boots up to her. "I borrowed those for you. I expect they'll be too big—our Highland lasses have braw feet—but if you spread your toes, you'll not leave them behind in the mud."

Jenna pulled them on, thrusting her own shoes into a capacious pocket of her jacket, and scrambled down from her perch to join him as he headed towards the house with the overseer.

"I know how Robinson Crusoe felt," she remarked feelingly, joining the two men.

"I hope you weren't too bored," said Ross.

"It was—grand," she answered, deliberately choosing a word she had heard often that morning.

"For a Sassenach you don't do badly," observed the overseer dryly.

"Oh, I'm learning the language," she laughed back. "I only wish I could roll my R's."

"It's a gift," he assured her, "given only to a chosen few."

The low door of the farmhouse stood open and a voice invited them in as they approached. An old-fashioned range burned brightly against one wall, and a plump woman turned from it as they entered.

"Come away in," she said. "There's tea on the hob and I've just made a batch of bannocks."*

---

*Flat, round or oval cakes, usually unleavened.

"You're an angel. How did you guess we'd be starved?"

She smiled at him indulgently. "Get away with you, Mr. Trent. Aren't you always troubled when you come out here?"

The tea was sweet, and stronger than Jenna cared for, but the hot oaty bannocks made up for that. She spread golden butter on them and ate more than she should until, sitting back replete, she licked the last of the melted butter from her fingers and sighed with contentment.

"I've never tasted anything so good," she said, and the farmer's wife flushed with pleasure, assuring her of a welcome and a plate of bannocks any time.

Soon after, Ross took his leave, reminding Jenna of the photographic session that afternoon. The overseer declined a lift, explaining that one of the men would bring him down later, and Ross and Jenna set off alone. They completed the short journey in silence and the girl was unhappily aware that her employer intended to keep his word about their relationship.

The photographer had already arrived and he joined them for lunch. A tall, thin, youngish man with a meagre amount of long wispy hair and an introspective manner, he seemed lost without a bevy of cameras hung around his neck and ate his meal almost in silence, only coming to life when Ross took him away to view the objects to be photographed.

Jenna had tried on the rose silk dress earlier and knew that it fitted her. Now she folded the sheet provided by Mrs. Frazer in half and, threading a length of tape along the fold, tied it around her waist, knowing from her acting experience at college that it would make a suitably full and heavy petticoat to suit the period of the dress. She slid the cool fold of the skirt over her head, then pushed her arms into the sleeves of the bodice. Holding her breath, she struggled to fasten the hooks and eyes lining the sides of the front opening. A creamy lace 'bertha',* found with the dress, covered the wide neckline like a deep collar, leaving most of her shoulders bare.

A different girl stared back at her from the mirror, dark eyes wide and almost nervous, quickened breath parting her lips and making her bosom rise and fall beneath the constricting corset.

Jenna wondered what to do about her hair and then combed it into smooth wings low on her cheeks, twisting it into a loose bun on the back of her head.

When she arrived in the balcony room, which had been chosen for the photography by reason of its light, she knew by Ross's expression and the sudden interest in the photographer's eyes that her efforts had been worthwhile.

A pale curtain had been hung against one wall and a high-backed Victorian chair placed for her. Obediently she sat down and arranged her skirts a little self-consciously.

"I'd like you to take this," said Ross. "Put it in your lap and look up and out—as if you'd just put it down."

She took the book from him, examining it with delight. Small and slim, but almost square in shape, it was covered in violet-coloured velvet, its pages edged with gold and a small gilt clasp fastening it together.

"Open it, if you will," came Ross's voice, while

---

*Woman's wide collar.

lights were arranged and directed at her. "And put it on your lap, with your left hand lightly resting across the pages."

She obeyed, though puzzled by the precise nature of his commands, and peered across the spotlights, trying to find the disembodied voice. The photographer adjusted the tilt of her head, a fold of her dress and the position of her hands with impersonal touches and then stepped back to examine the picture she made through his viewfinder. Apparently satisfied, he took several photographs.

Jenna dared to move and, shielding her eyes from the glaringly bright lights, looked down at the book in her lap. The spine gave no clue to its contents and, mildly curious, she examined it more closely. Cream brocade covered the inside of the boards and a neatly engraved bookplate had been glued on the inside of the front cover. For a moment the elegant spidery writing made no sense and she leaned closer while she made it out. Suddenly, her heart jumped against her tight, unaccustomed bodice and beat a tattoo under her ribs. She flung up her head and found Ross very near, coiling some wires and talking to the other man.

Unable to tell whether he had been watching her and was interested in her reaction to the book, she lowered her eyes and read the words again.

The Library of The Lady Silis MacKenzie

The copperplate danced before her eyes and she rubbed her fingers over the writing, smoothing the velvet and fingering the gilt fastening as she revelled in the fact that she was actually touching something that had belonged to her ancestress. Almost without volition the thought of the lost 'Luck' flew into her mind and she found herself making a promise to the elusive lady.

"I'll find it," she vowed silently. "I promise—I'll find it before I leave here."

Seventeen

She left the room while the men were still clearing the equipment away and climbed the stairs, her petticoats swirling about her ankles before she automatically bent and lifted her skirt, realizing how familiar the heavy clothes had become in the short while she had been wearing them. Not until she was in her room did she realize that she still held the violet book and, sitting down on the bed, she turned the leaves, glancing at the lines of poetry and at last recognizing them as Tennyson. A slip of paper slithered out and fluttered to the floor at her feet.

She bent to retrieve it, finding it crisp and brittle between her fingers. The writing was faded and brown, its letters unformed and childish. *To Dearest Mama*, she read, *from Jaimie and Alex.*

Thoughtfully she stared at the simple message, realizing all its implications. The book had been given to Silis by her sons, but it had obviously been privately bound. Who could have arranged such a long and expensive project? Not a governess or servant—of necessity it must have been the children's father ... but could someone who had arranged such a delicate emblem of affection have been as cold and hard as she imagined him? Reason made her begin to think differently of the lady's husband and, by the same reasoning, she must rethink her opinion of the Lady MacKenzie herself.

A perfunctory tap at the door recalled her to her surroundings and she absent-mindedly called "come in." Almost before she had spoken, the door opened and Carla appeared. Her eyes narrowed at the sight of Jenna's dress and she gave a hard, mirthless laugh.

"Why, how cute—you look like somebody's grandmother!"

"Did you want something?" Jenna asked coldly, sitting down at the dressing table and taking the pins out of her hair while she watched the other girl in the mirror.

"Only a few words—it's about time you and I had a little talk."

Jenna raised dark eyebrows and began to brush her hair, waiting for the other to continue.

Carla prowled around the room in her familiar way, staring out of the window at the terrace and sea below, touching the ornaments, picking up a book Jenna had been reading.

"You've made yourself quite at home," she commented. "I can't understand why Ross gave you this room, it's much too good for an employee."

"Perhaps you'd better ask him."

"I intend to—and another thing, honey, isn't it about time you started looking about for another position? Things will be different here in a little while." Carla came to stand behind Jenna, contemplating her reflection in the mirror and smoothing her brows with one finger. "I intend to make things quite different." She lowered her gaze deliberately to meet Jenna's and the younger girl flinched from the malice in her cold, blue eyes.

"But . . . I thought you were going back to America soon," she managed to say, while trying to take in the implications of the statement.

"Did you?" Carla swung away with a brittle laugh and went to sit on the bed, leaning against one elegant cornerpost while she regarded Jenna's back with a mixture of triumph and speculation.

"Aren't you leaving?" Jenna asked quietly, turning to look across the room as Carla hunted in her bag for cigarettes and lighter.

Inhaling smoke and tilting back her head, Carla looked at her through half-closed lids. "Well—promise you won't tell a soul—but Ross and I—" She broke off her calculated speech and Jenna knew what she was supposed to think.

"I see," she said miserably, and could only wonder why Carla had told her.

"And as you seemed a little keen on him yourself, he asked me to drop a hint. We wouldn't want you to get hurt."

There was no mistaking the meaning in her voice and Jenna raised her head to meet Carla's gaze steadily. "If things are so settled between you, Miss Van Damm, I can only wonder why you feel the need to warn me off."

Carla laughed. "Warn you off, darling! I was thinking of your own good. I know Ross only thinks of you as his secretary and any other ideas you might get would only make you unhappy."

"Well . . . thank you for bothering about me, but I'm quite capable of taking care of myself . . . and managing my own affairs."

For a moment both girls stared at each other and then Carla broke away, walking across the room and looking back, one hand on the door handle.

"I'm sure you know what I mean, Miss Clair. You wouldn't want me to make things uncomfortable for you." She smiled tightly and was gone, leaving Jenna to stare at the closed door.

Were Carla's insinuations true? she wondered,

and then remembered Ross's attentions to the American girl and how often she had been seen in his company.

Reason told her that it would be a most suitable match; they were socially equal, both rich and used to the good things of life. Comparing herself, she realized sadly how different was the life she had lived, and acknowledged in her heart that Ross would never have been interested in anyone as insignificant as herself.

With a flood of painful embarrassment, she recalled Carla's words and realized that they must have discussed her, that Ross was obviously only too aware of her feelings for him—and suddenly she knew that she could only face him again if she could prove that his suspicions were unfounded.

Unknowingly Alex proved her ally in this, eager and willing to flirt with her over dinner. His attentions were balm to her wounded pride and she responded happily, pleased to show Carla and Ross that they had been mistaken in their ideas of where her affections lay.

She agreed quickly when Alex suggested a walk along the beach and slipped her hand into his as they left the room. It seemed to her that Ross's eyes followed them and that he wasn't best pleased at her gesture, but she could only suppose that he thought her not good enough for his brother and she lifted her chin in a defiant manner as she caught his gaze.

She took the violet book with her next morning and, seeing him in his study as she passed, knocked lightly upon the open door.

"I took this with me by mistake yesterday," she explained, laying it down on his desk.

He looked up from the papers he was reading and, glancing briefly at her face, reached across and picked up the book. "Have you looked at it?"

"Yes . . . it's interesting."

"You noticed it belonged to the Lady Silis?"

She nodded, watching as he leafed through the pages and noticing how sharply his lean fingers showed brown against the thin yellowing paper. "I saw a note in it—it appears that her husband wasn't as cold as I've always thought him."

"Because he must have ordered it, you mean? I don't see why you have such a down on him. Of course we've always been on his side. After all, she was the one to run away, leaving her children behind. She's the villainess of the piece as far as we're concerned."

"Perhaps—but maybe they were both to blame. It takes two to make an unhappy marriage."

"Or a happy one." His eyes held hers and she felt a vivid flush run into her cheeks as she tried to look away from his grey gaze and hide her confusion from his penetrating glance.

"I've never cared for the Victorian poets, too lush and sentimental for my liking." At last he looked away and turned the slim volume around in his hands. "You keep it—you have an interest in my ancestress and the book is more suited to your tastes than mine."

She backed away as he held it out to her, confused and angry that he should offer her a present at that moment. "No—thank you," she said breathlessly, and crashed into the door as she moved back from the desk.

"Why ever not?" He really looked at her now, noticing the tears of anger on her cheeks.

"I—couldn't accept it, that's all," she answered shortly, fumbling at the door handle behind her.

"Why so prudish, Miss Clair? You've accepted presents from me before."

Goaded, she turned back. "Under the circumstances, I hardly think it was wise of you to offer them to me, Mr. Trent. Be sure that I shall have the greatest pleasure in refusing anything from you in the future." She flung the words at him, thrusting the book back across the desk. She had a glimpse of his face and momentarily wondered at his puzzled expression before she pulled open the door and dashed from the room.

Jenna flung herself into an orgy of work, spending her leisure hours in long walks or in Alex's company, persuading herself that she had never cared for Ross and that his brother more than made up for any lack of companionship she might have felt. Carla and Ross were much in each other's company and, by ill-founded chance, the two couples found themselves one evening due to dine out at the same hotel. The brothers arranged to drive in one car and, unable to disclose their true feelings, the two girls smiled sweetly and seethed inwardly.

Jenna wore a long white dress in soft jersey that she had made during the long winter evenings and had packed on the off chance that it would come in useful. She had embroidered a panel of brightly coloured flowers around the hem. That and a pair of jade earrings were her only ornaments.

Conscious that she looked her best, she smiled down at Alex where he waited at the foot of the stairs in the great hall. He seemed taller and older in dark blue evening clothes and he stretched out a hand to take her arm as she came down the last few steps.

"My, but you're beautiful!" he breathed admiringly. Then, as his fingers closed around hers, her heel slipped on the polished wood of the stair tread and with a startled cry she stumbled forward and was saved from a fall by his ready arms.

Finding herself held tightly against Alex's chest, Jenna lay still, not disliking the sensation. Before she knew what was happening his mouth closed gently over her own and, almost of their own volition, she found her lips responding to his kiss.

160

Crisp footsteps entered the hall and crossed the floor towards them, ringing on the stone flags. Almost guiltily they sprang apart, and Jenna at least was uncomfortably aware of Ross's disparaging eyes. Acutely conscious of his disapproval, she smoothed her hair and stared distractedly about at her surroundings, avoiding his gaze and generally giving the impression of embarrassment.

"Give Carla a call," her employer curtly commanded his brother, but at that moment the American girl appeared at the head of the stairs and, pausing for utmost effect, strolled elegantly down to meet them, her midnight blue satin gown catching the light with each movement.

"Have I kept you waiting?" she called gaily.

"If you have, it was worth every minute," said Ross gallantly, stepping forward to receive her hand on his arm and covering it with his own as they led the way from the hall.

Walking after them into the evening air, Jenna felt like an extra in a film, following behind the stars. All her happiness in her own outfit had faded when she saw Carla looking as glamourous as one of the old movie queens, and suddenly she felt that everyone would recognize the fact that her own dress was homemade.

The hotel was elegant and expensive, the meal superb—but might have consisted of dust and ashes for all Jenna noticed until, meeting Alex's worried gaze, she made an effort to enjoy herself for his sake. Shaking off her despondent mood, she joined in the conversation with an assumed gaiety, hoping no one else had noticed her silence.

Alex's frown cleared magically and he leaned closer. "Shall we dance?" he asked. "I'm not Fred Astaire, but I'm not too bad."

Smiling, she rose and, as he took her in his arms, found solace in the rhythm of the dance. Although he was shorter than his brother, she couldn't see over his shoulder and it wasn't until they swung around that she saw Ross and Carla were on the floor, too—his red head bent attentively over her blonde cap. Alex's arms closed tighter about her and soon they were lost among the other dancers.

"Big brother seems to be enjoying himself," he whispered in her ear, unknowingly adding to her pain. "I'd swear Carla is tightening her hooks." He glanced down at the unresponsive girl in his arms. "You're quiet, Jenna, are you tired?"

"A little—"

"Perhaps we should have come alone." He danced her over to where long curtains were drawn back from a pair of French windows. "Let's go outside. There's a good view of the town from up here."

He whisked her through the doors onto a wide terrace that was dotted with tables and chairs, and potted plants and shrubs. After the cigarette smoke and warm atmosphere of the crowded room, the slightly damp air was refreshing and he took her hand and led her to the parapet that edged the terrace.

The hotel was built on a hillside overlooking the town. Far below them, looking like a fairyland, the lights of houses and roads showed, the gleam of cars making ribbons in the dark night.

"There's always something special about being out at night, isn't there?" she sighed. "Like being allowed to stay up late as a child."

"We always stayed up to see the New Year in as children. I can still remember the delicious feeling of naughtiness as the clock struck."

She smiled up at him, sharing a moment of complete understanding. For a second his eyes stared down into hers and then his hands slid up her arms to her shoulders, caressing the warm skin of her neck. As his mouth hovered over hers, she

162

reached up and touched his lips with her fingers.

"Nothing serious, Alex," she warned gently.

His breath warmed her fingers. "This setting was made for romance," he whispered, "not seriousness."

And aware of the difference and knowing that he accepted her warning in the spirit in which it was given, she kissed him back, enjoying the romantic moment. Later, she was even able to accept with equanimity the sight of Ross and Carla close in each other's arms.

The car speeding home to Heron's Keep seemed a haven of security as she dozed against Alex's shoulder and she was almost sorry when they arrived in the courtyard. Ross tossed the keys to his brother, asking him to put away the car and he himself escorted the two girls up the steps and into the castle. Carla started up the stairs, but when Jenna would have followed, his quiet voice stopped her.

"A word with you, Miss Clair."

She stared at him sleepily. "N-now?" she asked bewildered.

"If you don't mind."

Drowsily, she followed his tall figure across the hall, wondering stupidly if he wanted her to take a letter at this time of night.

In his study he gestured her to a chair and, closing the door, leaned against it, his expression at once enigmatic and harsh.

"Doubtless you are aware that your contract has another two months to run. However, I find that I shall only need your services until the end of this month." Glancing down at her stricken face, he seemed to feel that something more was required. "Of course I shall pay you the full amount."

She made a curiously pathetic groping gesture and then let her hands fall back into her lap.

"You can take an unexpected holiday."

"Yes," she agreed tonelessly and, rising to her feet,

left him without another word, climbing the stairs with slow, dragging steps.

Away to her right a door closed, shutting off a shaft of light, and she knew that Carla had been waiting to see the outcome of her talk with Ross. Her own room was bathed in moonlight, bright silver reflecting back from the sea. But tonight the beauty of the scene had no attraction for her and she sat listlessly on the bed, too heartsore to even begin to undress. With dry eyes she stared ahead, and not until the dawn had begun to tinge the sky with grey did she fall asleep in the crumpled finery of the dress she had put on so happily only a few hours before.

Eighteen

Jenna was so preoccupied with her own thoughts during the succeeding days that it came as quite a shock to discover that the Fancy Dress Ball was less than a week away. All the invitations had been sent out some time ago and though Carla was often in consultation with Mrs. Frazer over the buffet supper and other arrangements, Jenna herself had hardly been involved lately.

Listlessly, she took out the rose taffeta she had bought to make a replica of the Victorian dress she had worn for the photographs, but all her interest and enthusiasm had faded and, wrapping it again, she pushed it to the back of her cupboard and moodily stared out of the window.

Ross Trent's history of Heron's Keep was almost ready for the publishers. She knew by heart how Jaimie and Alexander had spent their lives, seeming not to notice the loss of their mother. How Jaimie had married Carla's grandmother's sister . . . and how her American fortune had refilled the Trent's empty coffers. She had to admit to herself that it was remarkably well-written, only the chapter on the MacKenzie 'Luck' being thin and unsatisfying . . . and again there was that elusive memory, tugging at the back of her mind. Something, somewhere—recently—connected with it that she should remember.

The next few days passed quickly, she hardly saw Carla and Alex, and Ross had left the morning after the disastrous double date and wouldn't be back until the day of the ball. Half of her was relieved at his absence, but the other knew that she wouldn't be seeing much more of him and regretted any time lost.

The day of the ball arrived and wandering down into the hall, she found Mrs. Frazer just closing the door after receiving two huge boxes from the costume rental firm.

"Shall I take them up for you?" she offered, noticing the enveloping apron and smudge of flour on the housekeeper's face.

"I'd be grateful if you would." Mrs. Frazer looked around at the men perched on ladders, replacing the cleaned chandeliers, and glanced through the open door of the dining room where a long table was being set for the cold supper. "There's that much to do. We've women in from the village, but I could do with another pair of hands."

"Let me help—I've nothing to do."

The older woman looked at her. "Well . . . if you really mean it, Miss, I'd be grateful," she answered doubtfully.

"I'll just take these upstairs and then come down into the kitchen," Jenna assured her, eager to have something to take her mind off her troubles.

She put one box on the bed in Carla's room and then hurried away from the oppressive atmosphere which was heavy with expensive perfume, and hesitated before opening the door into her employer's room. It seemed full of its owner's personality—almost as though Ross was there in person—and she hastily thrust the other box on the table and went down to the kitchens.

"Now, what shall I do?" she asked with assumed

cheerfulness, as the housekeeper tied a huge apron around her trim waist.

"There are pastry boats and cases to be filled and decorated, if you'd like to do that." She showed Jenna where everything was and then returned to the stove where she was making last minute sauces and fondues.

Jenna rather enjoyed her task, using all her artistic imagination to arrange the savoury tidbits and fruit flans and trifles.

"No doubt you'll be wearing something pretty tonight," Mrs. Frazer remarked, plying her wooden spoon vigorously.

"I did intend making myself a dress—but somehow I've never got around to it."

The housekeeper looked up, her shrewd eyes taking in the weary droop of the girl's shoulders and the dark shadows under her eyes. "If you ask me, you've been working too hard," she said severely. "And now, I suppose you've nothing to wear."

Jenna shook her head. "I don't think I'll go. No one will miss me."

"Nonsense! I know Mr. Alex is expecting you to be there. To give him confidence, he says, though why a grown man should be afraid of a bit of dressing up, I don't know." She stirred thoughtfully for a while and then, after glancing across at Jenna a few times, suddenly said, "Now—I've an idea. My girl Meg is a great one for dancing. She's won cups and ribbons galore. And I know she's got a Highland costume tucked away in a cupboard somewhere here. You're just about her size—if you'd care to wear it."

"A Highland costume?" repeated Jenna cautiously.

Mrs. Frazer snorted. "Oh, I know fine what you're thinking—a kilt and a velvet jacket! Well, I'll have you know they're men's clothes and no self-respecting lassie would be seen in them. I've in mind a braw tartan skirt, with a white blouse and a black velvet bodice."

"It sounds very nice—"

"I'll sort them out when I have time and pop them into your room," said the housekeeper as though all was settled, and somehow Jenna was relieved to have the decision of whether or not to go to the ball taken out of her hands.

And when later that evening she was dressed in the short skirt, crisp full-sleeved blouse and tightly laced black bodice, she knew it suited her. Leaving her hair loose, she pinned the length of tartan material over one shoulder with a silver brooch. Then, glancing at her reflection in the mirror, she left the room, remembering that Ross had asked that they all be ready in the great hall to greet the guests as they arrived.

Alex was already there when she descended the stairs and she smiled to see him prowling restlessly about.

"You look super," she assured him truthfully, for the full Highland evening dress he had elected to wear—as being in keeping with the ball, but more acceptable to him than fancy dress—fitted him to perfection.

Smoothing his velvet jacket, he eyed her with approval. "And you make a braw Highland lassie yourself."

"Mrs. Frazer lent it to me. It's her daughter's. Do you know whose tartan it is?"

"Ours, Miss Clair," came a voice from above. "You're wearing the MacKenzie tartan."

Startled, she looked up to find herself staring at the original of the portrait in the Tudor room. Ross Trent was wearing trews and a short frogged and braided jacket, crossed with a plaid that matched her skirt. A gay cap was set at a jaunty angle on his red head. Her heart leaped at sight of him and involuntarily her hand sprang to cover its beating from his gaze.

"Will I do?" came Carla's cool voice, assured of their answer as she posed at the head of the stairs, elegant in a cream Edwardian evening dress. A diamond choker glittered at her throat and three ostrich feathers nodded in her upswept hair.

Jenna had to admit that she was breathtakingly beautiful and, for once, was glad of her spectacular entrance, as it meant that she herself could retire into the background and observe without being noticed.

Soon guests began to arrive and quickly the hall was filled with clowns and courtesans, pirates and pierrettes, characters from history and plays—and wild combinations of all, some of whom could have come from outer space. Jenna found herself claimed by an Arab, and then by a Cavalier, and after that she never wanted for a partner. Almost in spite of herself she began to enjoy the evening, finding balm for her damaged spirits in her partners' pleasure in her company and in their outrageous flirting.

Alex took her in to supper and then was lost in a Paul Jones. Finding herself alone for a moment, she retired thankfully to a seat and sank down to watch the more energetic guests fling themselves happily into a lively modern dance. Suddenly the music changed and became the measured tempo of a Viennese waltz with the dancers a dipping, swaying mass of colour.

"Our dance, Miss Clair," said a voice, and Jenna looked up to meet the cool grey eyes of her employer.

"Oh—no thank you!" she murmured, shrinking back against the soft cushions and wishing she was anywhere but sitting helpless in front of the determined Ross Trent.

Ignoring her refusal he held out his hand and,

when she didn't respond, took her wrist in a steely grip and pulled her to her feet. "No wallflowers in my house, Jenna Clair," he told her and took her in his arms.

The touch of his hand on her back seemed to scorch through her dress. Never, it seemed, had she been held so close before . . . and he had called her Jenna. . . .

They moved as one, their steps so in tune that the dance seemed to Jenna almost like flying. Ross whirled her around the room—and then before she knew, or could protest, he whisked her under a curtain and through a door into one of the many corridors that lined the castle's ancient walls.

"I've something to show you," he said briefly in answer to her look of inquiry and, with a firm hand on her waist, led her into his study.

"Stay there," he commanded, placing her in front of his desk and going behind it to lift a heavy object wrapped in thick brown paper. Untying the string with maddening deliberation, he wound it around his fingers and placed it in his pocket. Jenna felt bound to point out that his guests would miss him.

"Not for a while," was the brief answer as the wrapping paper fell away to disclose another covering of several layers of soft linen.

Jenna watched fascinated as the wrappings dropped away and moved closer. A picture in a large, black oval frame was revealed.

"This is by Josef Laurens Dykmans—he painted it while he was over here exhibiting at the Royal Academy in about 1860, or so. It's on loan to a museum . . . I've just been to collect it." He blocked her view as he stood it on a table, propping it against the wall. At last he stood back and reached a long arm for the girl. "Now, Miss Clair, tell me what you think," he said, pulling her in front of him and holding her firmly there, a hand on either shoulder.

Jenna gazed at the woman in the rose silk gown, recognizing the dress first and then something familiar—more than familiar—in the pale face framed by wings of smooth, dark hair. She looked more closely, stared doubtfully and then with growing amazement.

"Who is it?" she whispered, drawing back, feeling the man behind her and glad of his strength.

"I think you know."

"The . . . Lady?"

"Silis MacKenzie, painted in the year she ran away with the overseer from Glen Clair." He felt the girl draw away, her shoulders tense under his hands, and gently turned her to face him. Imprisoning her chin, he tilted her face up to meet his eyes. "I think the time has come to tell me who you are," he said and felt her shiver at the inexorable tone of his voice.

He stared down into her eyes, wide and dark with something strangely vulnerable in their depths, and shook her slightly, almost caressingly. "Jenna—Jenna," he said softly.

The girl moved at the sound of her name, knowing that she must break free at once or she would tell him whatever he wanted to know. He quelled her struggles easily, almost negligently, merely tightening his grip until she realized the futility of her efforts and stood still.

"You're descended from her, aren't you?" he asked quietly, his breath stirring her hair. "And I imagine, from your defense of her, that you thought you'd find that Heron's Keep should have been yours."

Realizing the foolishness of her ambitions, she nodded dumbly. "My father—we all thought that *we* were the real owners—"

"And that the Trents were usurpers. How romantic!"

She lifted her head at the dry note in his voice. "It sounds silly, I know. Things like that don't happen now, but the Lady was our ancestress and we were all nurtured on tales about her. How she escaped, leaving her wealth and lands, and willing to be poor for the sake of the man she loved. I suppose over the years the unromantic parts got left out. I'd never heard about her marriage or her sons or that she was . . . and that we were . . ."

His lips curved at the half-swallowed sob in her voice and, when he saw the tears glittering on her lashes, he folded her gently in his arms, with one hand making her look up so that he could see her face.

"Why keep it a mystery?" he asked. "Why did you let me suspect all kinds of things about you?"

"How could I tell you—I thought of you as one of the wicked Trents who'd taken our inheritance. Besides . . . we didn't exactly hit it off on the right foot to begin with. I spent a long time hating you."

He laughed. "And most of the time I've either wanted to shake you—or kiss you!"

She looked up quickly, wide-eyed with surprise. And, seizing the opportunity presented, Ross bent his head to cover her mouth with his. His lips were firm and cool but, as Jenna gave herself up to the kiss, they became warm and demanding. Breathless, she hung in his arms, her whole being responding as his grip tightened. At last he lifted his head and looked at her, a tender, quizzical smile touching his mouth. "I—think we have both wanted that for some time."

Jenna hid her flushed cheeks against his gay blue jacket, but one hand slid up and curved around his neck. His fingers closed over that hand, carrying it to his lips, his eyes glinting down at her.

She sighed and nestled closer, content to rest

upon his strength until, aware that he was gently disentangling himself, her eyes flew to his face.

"We'd better go back to the great hall," he said quietly. "I've my guests to look after and the ball will be breaking up soon."

He slid a finger down her short nose and touched her mouth caressingly. "Tomorrow," he promised. "I'll see you tomorrow."

And with that she had to be content. She returned to mix with the guests, only too conscious of Carla's icy, blue eyes following her, until at last the ball was over and Heron's Keep was peaceful and quiet again. Jenna helped a tired but triumphant Mrs. Frazer tidy a few things and then slipped away to bed, a haze of happiness welling inside her as she recalled the scene in Ross's study. He had called her by name and had held her close—and kissed her. She smiled sleepily at the memory, and then her eyes flew open in the darkness, suddenly wide-awake. To be sure, he had kissed her and promised a meeting the next day. But not a word of love or even affection had been spoken. With sickening clarity, she recalled Carla's prior claim on him . . . and with the memory of the American girl, all desire for sleep left her.

She lay watching the moonlight creep across the pale carpet, making black and frightening shadows on the floor—and for the first time Heron's Keep seemed a lonely, alien place.

Nineteen

Breakfast next morning was a leisurely, informal meal, as they each came into the kitchen and helped themselves to whatever was available. Jenna pecked at a bowl of cereal and drank a cup of sweet, black coffee before wandering back into the hall.

Her heart leaped at the sight of Ross bursting from his study. He paused when he saw her and hesitated long enough to say hastily, "I've just had a phone call from MacKenzie—something's happened and he needs me. Jenna—" his voice changed and he half put out a hand to her. "I've . . . written you a note and put it under your door. I didn't expect you to be up this early. I put it under your door—I'm sorry it has to be this way—"

Jenna watched as he hurried from the hall, gazing after him out of the open door. Slowly she climbed one step of the stairs, pausing with a hand on the round top of the newel post as his car started. As the engine died away, she continued on up, finding a square envelope at her feet when she opened her bedroom door.

Bending, she picked it up, feeling the thick paper and staring at the well-known angular writing.

"A billet-doux, my pet?"

Carla's eyes were bright and angry as she looked at the envelope in Jenna's hand, obviously recognizing the unmistakable writing. "What *can* Ross have to say—after the length of time you kept him in his study last night?"

"I won't know until I read it, will I?" Jenna said sweetly. "If you'll excuse me—" Stepping inside her room, she closed the door firmly and, crossing to the window, tore open the envelope.

The letter began at once without a heading or inscription, and she skimmed through it quickly and then again more slowly, biting her lip as she took in the meaning.

> *My apologies for last night. I can only say that the circumstances and surroundings got the better of us and we forgot our commitments and duty to others. Rest assured that the incident is forgotten as far as I am concerned, and that I shall put all thought of the matter out of my mind—and hope that you feel able to do the same.*

Lifting her head, she stared blankly out at the bright sky, crumpling the note as her fingers unconsciously tightened in her lap. She could only suppose he meant Carla when he spoke of commitments and duty, and had to acknowledge sadly that he obviously thought of the interlude in his study the night before as just a moment's madness— something not worth a second thought.

With the history of the castle finished and only a little general tidying up left to do, she knew in a second that to stay at the castle and be forced to meet Ross day after day would be too painful, and she decided to finish her work and ask to be allowed to leave at once.

She was on her way to her workroom and just crossing the hall when Carla called, the note of near panic in her voice making the other girl hurry into the balcony room.

"I've got something in my eye," said the American, her face half-hidden behind both her hands. "Could you run upstairs to my room and find a handkerchief? They're in a drawer in the dressing table."

"Of course," Jenna ran upstairs and, without thinking that her own was nearer, obeyed the command and hurried into Carla's room.

Hesitating irresolutely in front of the bow-shaped dressing table, she wondered which drawer to choose; then kneeling, she tugged out first one and then another, rummaging hastily through their contents.

"Did you want something, miss?" Mrs. Frazer stood in the interior doorway. By the cloths and cleaning materials in her hands, she had obviously been tidying Carla's bathroom. She eyed Jenna uncertainly. "Are you looking for something?"

"Yes—a handkerchief. Miss Van Damm has got something in her eye."

"Well, you'll not find them there—she keeps her handkerchiefs over here." She went to a small chest of drawers and, taking out a square of linen, handed it to Jenna.

"But—I thought she said—Never mind, it doesn't matter. I'll take it to her."

Carla appeared to have recovered when Jenna ran into the balcony room and, tucking the small lacy square into her sleeve, remarked that whatever it was it had gone.

A little puzzled, Jenna went back to her work and soon had the satisfaction of knowing that if she worked hard all afternoon, her tasks would be done and she could ask to leave with a clear conscience. Her decision brought a lifting of her spirits and she began to move almost eagerly about the room, tidying files and checking papers.

But still tense, her fingers were stiff and clumsy and suddenly a file slipped through her hands, shedding its contents across the floor. With a muttered exclamation she knelt to retrieve them and paused, one hand outstretched, as she stared down at some writing that seemed to leap up at her—

to find the MacKenzie 'Luck' for it is ever at hand, safe under the badge of the clan—

Her breath caught in her throat, her heartbeat sending a pulse jumping as she realized at last that she knew where to look for the missing 'Luck'. The elusive memory had returned and she knew that she had touched the hiding place that very day. Scrambling to her feet, she ran into the hall and, mounting the first step, stared at the newel post and the carving that had grown familiar over the last few months.

Seizing it in both hands she twisted with all her strength, but to no avail. Almost crying with frustration, she jumped down, looking about for something, someone to help her. And hearing sounds of a man's voice coming from the kitchen, she pushed open the door and saw Euan MacKenzie in conversation with the housekeeper.

"Thank goodness! Do come quickly," Jenna cried, clutching his arm and almost dragging him from the room. "Can you unscrew the top of the newel post?" she asked urgently, giving him an impatient push towards the stairs.

"I'll try," he said slowly, and without more ado strode across the hall. Taking the post in both hands he gave it a trial twist and then, bunching his shoulders, used all his strength.

Jenna watched his mouth tighten and his arms tremble slightly with effort and she held her own breath in sympathy. Suddenly he grunted in triumph and, his face relaxing, he shot her a quick smile and swiftly unscrewed the huge, wooden ball.

"There you are, miss," he said, "though what good it'll do you, I don't know."

Quickly she examined the ball and, finding it uncompromisingly solid, turned her attention to the base of the post. At once she saw a small, but fairly deep hole in the centre, with what looked like a roll of cloth in its depths. Stretching her fingers to their limits she could just touch it and, with an effort, managed to catch her nails under a cord and pull it out of its hiding place.

"What is it, Miss Clair?" asked the housekeeper, who had been a curious watcher all the while.

"I'm—not sure," said Jenna moved by some impulse to keep her find a secret until she could have the triumph of handing it to her employer. "I'll show you later." Turning on her heels, she ran quickly up the stairs. Glancing back from the head of the stairs, she saw the overseer swing around and leave the hall, while Mrs. Frazer gazed from here to there in bewilderment.

Once safely in her own room, Jenna dared to look at what she held and discovered that she was clutching a small leather bag, drawn up with string at the neck, and sadly discoloured with age. Holding her breath, she carefully opened it with fingers that trembled slightly. Feeling something hard and smooth, she drew it out—and for the first time in nearly a century the 'Luck' of the MacKenzies shone dully in the daylight.

About the size of a small egg—opaque, but with flakes of gold in it—it lay on the palm of her hand, cold and heavy in its antiquity. For a few seconds she stared at it and then, hearing Carla's strident voice raised loudly in the hall, she thrust it back in its bag. Hastily opening a drawer, she hid it among her handkerchiefs. Just in time, she moved away and was standing near the window when the American girl burst in.

"Where is it?" she demanded, advancing into the centre of the room and looking around. She went on with an attempt at conciliation. "Mrs. Frazer told me that you'd found something in the post of the stairs and I can guess what it is. You'd better give it to me to look after—after all, I am family."

"Somehow I don't feel you'd look after it too well," said Jenna, glad to be able to discard subterfuge and at last say what she really felt. "I'll keep it, just in case you feel a sudden inclination to leave for the States!"

"Now, see here, honey," hissed Carla, her eyes narrow and dangerous as she advanced upon the other girl. "I've had just about enough of you. Give the 'Luck' to me and I'll say nothing about you trying to keep it—I'll even help you to get away from here before Ross comes back."

"Thanks—but I've a good reason for seeing Mr. Trent," answered Jenna, suddenly sure that her suspicions regarding Carla's intentions towards the 'Luck' were true.

"Don't try my patience too far, you little ninny," Carla advised, her voice charged with menace. "You'll be sorry if you don't do as I say."

Jenna faced her, a cold anger growing. "What will you do?" she asked. "I assure you that the days of private dungeons and prisoners are long over. You might be rich, but your wealth can do nothing to me. I'm not afraid of you, Miss Van Damm, and I'll do as I please—not as you say."

"I warn you—"

"I'm rather tired of this—neither do I care for your company. I find you boring and totally uninteresting. Please leave my room."

Goaded into an uncontrollable rage, Carla's arm

flashed out and her open hand caught Jenna sharply on the cheek. Instinctively, she struck back and her fingers tangled in the long, blonde tresses of her opponent—just as the door opened and a voice inquired coldly what was happening.

Both girls stiffened, quieting under the authority of Ross's gaze. Then Carla sprang across the room and flung herself against his chest.

"Oh, Ross honey, am I glad you came! She—she attacked me!"

"I didn't," Jenna cried indignantly. "She hit me."

"Be quiet, both of you," Ross snapped and, putting Carla aside, he leaned against the wall, folding his arms, his eyes cold as he looked at them. "Now tell me calmly what happened."

"I hardly like to," began Carla, drooping her head until her face was hidden by the fall of golden hair, but her voice effectively drowned Jenna's softer tones. "I missed my gold bangle this afternoon and—and looked all over for it."

Jenna eyed her, wondering where she was leading.

"I—remembered seeing Miss Clair coming out of my room this morning and, knowing that she had no cause to be there, I wondered— Oh, Ross, it's too horrible!" She bit back a sob, covering her face with her hands and giving a display that everyone except Jenna seemed to find convincing.

"What does Miss Clair say?" asked Ross over her head.

"I . . . was there, but she asked me to find a handkerchief for her—she had something in her eye." Jenna answered lamely, realizing helplessly that the American girl must have arranged all this.

Carla spoke in a muffled tone. "Oh, Miss Clair, how could you?" She turned to Ross. "That's simply not true."

"Mrs. Frazer was there," put in the other girl desperately.

The man raised his eyebrows and asked the housekeeper for her confirmation.

"I was there when Miss Clair came in—or at least I heard her rummaging in the dressing table and wondered who it could be."

"Well . . . that proves it, then. If I'd told her to find me a handkerchief I'd have told her where to look. I keep them in the small chest."

Ross looked from her to the other girl, while Jenna felt her face drain of colour. Unable to find words to express her feelings, she wondered if she'd ever recover her voice.

"The easiest way would be to look," went on Carla, something in her voice making Jenna raise her head warily. A concealed note of triumph and excitement told her that the affair was going the way Carla wanted. "I found her closing that drawer over there when I came in."

Jenna followed her pointing finger and realized with dismay that she was indicating the very drawer where the 'Luck' was hidden. At last she found her voice and, starting forward with a strangled cry, placed herself in front of the dressing table.

Ross pushed himself away from the wall and came towards her. "Move aside, Miss Clair," he said quietly, and with both hands on her shoulders he gently pushed her away.

She watched helplessly as his brown hands searched among her handkerchiefs, touched something and drew it out . . . then found another object and displayed them both on his open palm for her to see. A wild flush ran up her fair skin and she gasped with shock, knowing she must appear guilty. She blinked back the tears and tried to face him calmly.

"There—is some mistake—"

"About the bracelet, I'll keep an open mind. But the 'Luck', Miss Clair? MacKenzie told me what you'd found and I came at once, expecting you to give it to me. Instead I find that you'd hidden it. I think that needs some explanation."

"She's obviously a kleptomaniac," put in Carla, unable to keep the pleasure out of her voice.

Jenna ignored her. She had caught sight of Ross's expression and all assurance that he would believe her was slowly dying. His eyes were cold and bleak, and he looked at her without a hint of warmth. He might have been a stranger.

"Please—" she whispered, putting out a hand as though they were the only ones in the room.

Ignoring her gesture, he looked down at her, his mouth set. And something in his expression made her tremble. "I'm waiting," he said inexorably.

Suddenly she could bear no more. Whether she was thought guilty of stealing or not, ceased to matter. The only important thing was to get away from that room and the accusing faces. With a half-smothered sob, she brushed Ross aside and dashed out of the room and down the stairs. Stumbling and almost falling in her tearful haste, she ran out into the courtyard, stared blindly around for a moment, then jumped into her car and started the engine.

Twenty

The tires shrieked as she swung the wheel, pulling the car under the archway and out onto the road. Without hesitation, like an animal running for home, she turned to the left and pressed her foot down hard on the accelerator, unheeding of her speed, only realizing the need to get away from Heron's Keep. The track to Glen Clair came into view and, instinctively, she spun the wheel and headed along the winding road, the uneven surface forcing her to slow her speed a little.

Sheep bounded away as the car bounced and bucked around pot holes and between boulders. Jenna clutched the wheel, pitting her wits and meagre skill against the rough track and straining car. A movement behind caught her eye in the driving mirror and she frowned as she recognized Ross's big Land Rover turn onto the Glen Clair road.

Her hands tightened as she pushed down the accelerator pedal, feeling her speed mount again as the speedometer needle quivered uncertainly. The other vehicle made no effort to gain on her smaller car, being content to follow at a distance. And when the ruined croft appeared Jenna realized the reason: in her hurry and distress, she had quite forgotten that the track ended beside the broken cottage.

Skidding on the loose shingle, she slammed on the brakes and, the minute the car had stopped, opened the door and jumped out. For a moment she stood irresolute; she started towards the croft and then changed her mind and ran in the direction of the nearest hill, following a faint, undulating path that led among the boulders and high tussocks of grass and heather.

Splashing through tea-brown puddles that lay unsuspected under her feet, and skirting large white stones and startled sheep, she soon realized that the path she had chosen had not been made by humans but by the small feet of animals. Glancing behind she saw that the Land Rover had stopped beside her own car and its driver had gotten out and stood watching her. Even as she looked, he started off in pursuit, a loud shout echoing around the enclosing mountains and making her take to her heels again.

The path under her flying feet began to mount upwards, and soon her run slowed to a walk and then to a crawl as she was forced to bend her back and look for hand-holds among the shale and rocks ahead. Quickly, all vestige of the path was gone and she found herself climbing the almost perpendicular rock face.

Suddenly the way ahead seemed impassable and, lifting her head, she panted while searching for a path. Her scrabbling hands touched a mass of small, loose stones and a stream of shale started sliding towards her feet. Losing her footing, she began to slide downwards and, fighting to regain her balance, she flung herself against the rock, clinging to its rough surface. Panic-stricken, she fell to her knees, her fingers clutching among the crevices, heedless of scratches and broken nails.

"Come down," commanded a voice below her, and Jenna turned her head against her shoulder to look at Ross standing on the path where it dissolved among the fallen boulders and scree.*

"That's just what I'm trying not to do," she quavered, and, finding a small crack level with her nose, she wedged her fingers into it and closed her eyes with relief.

"Come down, you silly girl," Ross repeated. But having found security, however illusory, Jenna had no intention of vacating it just because the man below told her to. Shaking her head resolutely, she stayed where she was.

And exasperated sigh carried up to her, and sounds of boots against stone and the slither of a climbing body came nearer, until the man's head came into view under her arm. Jenna looked at him coldly and turned away as he drew level with her precarious perch.

"Let go and put your feet down—there's a safe foothold about two feet below you."

"No," she whispered, and crouched lower against the rock.

Ross eyed her doubtfully, noticing the signs of near panic and strain before he reached an arm across her, letting her feel it firm and strong over her shoulders.

"Jenna, my love, you don't think I'd let you fall, do you?" he asked in her ear. "Come on, try now—you can trust me." And slowly, under his persuasion, the girl responded to his instructions. At last, they were safe on the gentler slopes below. At once his manner changed and rounding on her, he seized her shoulders in both his hands and shook her violently.

"You silly little fool!" he snarled, "you might have killed yourself."

---

*Mass of loose rock fragments at the bottom of a cliff or on a mountainside.

Jenna's head snapped backwards under the force of the unexpected attack and her mouth opened wide with surprise—before her temper broke with the strain of the last few hours and her hand flew out towards the angry face above her, her fingers stretched like talons.

Her wrist was caught, fingers closing with bruising force about her slender bones and she was jerked roughly against his chest. Holding both her hands in a painful grip, he glared down at her as she lashed out at his shins with each foot.

"Let me go!" she panted squirming in his arms, her hair breaking free of its confining ribbon and falling in a soft cloud about her shoulders. "I hate you, Ross Trent—I hate you!"

His eyes gleamed and he changed his hold, letting go her hands but pulling her close before she could pull away. Ruthlessly tilting up her chin, he smiled a little cruelly down into her eyes. "No, you don't," he said. "You don't hate me at all."

Once before she had felt his kiss, but this was different. His lips were hard and demanding, his teeth grating against hers as he held her head still with his fingers spread under her chin and against her cheek.

She fought wildly, her temper still high, but her strength was useless against his and at last she was still, exhausted and trembling in his arms. And now his kiss changed, his lips finding hers were gentle and she was responding. Then she drew back, shaken by the force of her feelings.

"To hell with duty!" he exploded suddenly. "You don't love Alex!"

Her eyes widened, dark and vulnerable above her soft, bruised mouth. "Love Alex!" she repeated blankly. "Why should I love Alex?"

His grasp slackened and, putting her away from him, he looked down into her eyes, still holding her with his hands on her upper arms. "I thought that you and Alex—"

She shook her head. "No—never! Oh, I like him and find him attractive—but not in that way." He would have pulled her back into his arms then, but she put out a hand and held him off. "Aren't you forgetting Miss Van Damm?" she asked, trying to speak coldly. But while she waited for his reply her heart began to beat against her ribs.

"Carla? Why should I?" He laughed suddenly and, reaching out a long arm, pulled her against him. "Did you think I cared for that rich, spoiled miss?"

"She gave me that impression."

"I think Miss Van Damm is about to cut short her visit to Heron's Keep," he said grimly. "I've suspected that young lady of shady dealings for some time, and I've just told her so in no uncertain terms. When I left, Mrs. Frazer was helping her to pack." He pinched Jenna's chin between his thumb and forefinger, making her meet his eyes. "Now, tell me, if you please, just what you intended to do with the 'Luck'?"

Shyly, she looked at him, wondering why she had never noticed the different shades of colour in his grey eyes before. "You didn't really think I was stealing it?"

"Not for a moment—"

"But you sounded so angry . . . and looked so cold."

"I'd just realized that Carla had framed you and was having difficulty in keeping my hand from that young madam's bottom. I could have wrung her neck when I saw the mark where she'd slapped you."

She looked at him wonderingly. "I thought you were attracted to her—you were always together, taking her out, and dancing and talking with her."

"And you were always with Alex," he accused.

"Yes—well," she hung her head. "I wanted to show that I didn't care about you and Carla," she confessed. "And perhaps I did try to make you a little jealous."

"You succeeded," he acknowledged between his teeth. "And you gave me some pretty worrying moments. I knew right from the first that I'd seen you—or someone very like you—somewhere before. And when I saw you in the pink dress that I bought for you, I remembered the picture of the Lady."

"That was strange," she said soberly. "So like me—and yet all those years and people between. I wondered why you arranged me so carefully for the photograph."

"I'll set them together on the same page . . . no doubt the readers will like the coincidence." For a moment longer he looked down at her as though unwilling ever to stop. Then he dropped one hand and gently turned her to face back the way they had come. "Time we headed for the castle," he said, putting an arm round her shoulders and tucking her comfortably in against his side.

"Poor lady," Jenna sighed as they passed the ruins of the cottage.

"I hope she and her crofter were happy."

"I'm sure they were—I expect the world was well lost for their love."

He hugged her. "You're incurably romantic," he laughed. "How do you think she liked slaving over a hot range and doing the weekly wash, when she'd known servants all her life?"

"I expect she thought to be loved was worth it," the girl replied stoutly.

"And—will you, Jenna?"

She stopped and slowly turned to face him, her eyes searching his face. The slanting sun sent shadows across the planes of his face, touching fire to his hair and making his eyes return the light. Jenna's lips parted slightly and her breath came unevenly—while behind them, the still solid walls of the croft seemed to wait silently for an answer.

Carrying her bruised hands to his mouth, he lightly kissed each scratched fingertip. "You must make an answer, you know," he said gently.

Taking a breath, she said simply, "If you love me."

"Haven't I told you so?" he teased.

She shook her head. "Not yet."

"Jenna—Jenna." He caught her to him, holding her with strong arms and, at last, he said, "Jenna, I love you—do you think you could bear to spend the rest of your life with the ogre in his castle?"

With her soul in her eyes, Jenna raised her head. "Ross . . . yes!" she breathed.

Lifting her off her feet, he spun around and shouted with exultation. "Jenna Clair, I love you!"

"Love you—love you," came back in echo from the encircling mountains and for a moment they both lifted their heads and listened. Then, laughing, they ran hand in hand the few yards to the cars.

"I'll come with you," said Jenna, unwilling to be parted even for the short journey to the castle. She scrambled in beside him.

Ross started the engine and turned to look at her for a second. "Let's go home, my love," he said huskily, and kissed her quickly before starting the Land Rover along the track.

Soon Heron's Keep came into view, standing solid and foursquare upon its rock. The road led like a ribbon to the grey stone archway, seeming to lead them home and, with a feeling of content, Jenna tucked her hand into Ross's elbow.

The road dropped down towards the castle and familiar entrance. Stopping the car in the courtyard, Ross turned to look steadily at her, his expression tender and meaningful.

"Welcome home, Jenna Clair," he said softly. And as their lips met, Jenna was sure that somewhere the Lady Silis knew and smiled with them.

ABOUT THE AUTHOR

Samantha Clare was born and brought up in Portsmouth, England, and is now living in a small village in Scotland, where her husband keeps the shop and the post office.

Samantha has two children—a son of twenty-one in the army, and a thirteen-year-old daughter who is still at school.

She has written since childhood and has had five novels of various types published under different names—the first in 1973.

Her interests are history, folk legends and stories, music, books, theater—and tapestry work.

She likes people, animals, the countryside, and being in the open. She dislikes bigotry of any kind, being enclosed—and noise first thing in the morning.

CIRCLE OF LOVE

Step out of your world and enter the Circle of Love.

Six new CIRCLE OF LOVE romances are available every month. Here's a preview of the six newest titles on sale May 15, 1982:

#16 INNOCENT DECEPTION by Anne Neville (#21516-7 • $1.75)

It was a chance for Laurel to taste a life of unaccustomed luxury. But little did she realize the consequences of impersonating her glamorous, coldhearted twin sister—or how her own heart would betray her once she was thrust into the arms of Derek Clayton, her sister's estranged but wealthy husband.

#17 PAMELA by Mary Mackie (#21505-1 • $1.75)

Pamela woke in a hospital room with no memory of her past, no knowledge of her name. Her only thought was of her instant attraction to the hostile and handsome man before her. Pamela did not recall anything he told her of her past...and even worse, she felt herself plunging headlong into careless desire for this dangerously seductive man.

#18 SAND CASTLES by Alexandra Kirk (#21529-9 • $1.75)

Jason Kent always got what he wanted. And now he wanted Melissa to give up her independence and become governess to his young, motherless daughter. But could she cope with the desires which welled up in her heart when Jason was near? And could she stand to be so close to him—and watch him marry another woman?

#19 THE WISHING STONE by Jean Innes
(#21518-3 • $1.75)

Katie Boswell had no qualms about giving up her city life—no regrets about becoming her widowed aunt's young companion. But why must Aunt Vee insist on playing the matchmaker—calling upon the ancient powers of the Wishing Stone to make her dreams for Katie come true?

#20 THE TEMPESTUOUS AFFAIR
by Margaret Fletcher (#21501-9 • $1.75)

Their first meeting had been stormy; their second, a shock. But now Vivienne Scott stood beside Julian Garston—the father of the man she was engaged to marry—and knew she loved him. But no one else must ever know.

#21 CIRCLES OF FATE by Anne Saunders
(#21522-1 • $1.75)

Anita was confused. No, overwhelmed! She had come to Isla de Leyenda—The Island of Legend—to see Casa Esmeralda, her mother's ancestral home and to meet Edward. She should be happy, yet all she could think of was another man—a man she hardly knew!